THE
BOXMAKER'S
SON

THE
BOXMAKER'S
SON

DONALD S. SMURTHWAITE

DESERET
BOOK

SALT LAKE CITY, UTAH

DESERET BOOK is a registered trademark of Deseret Book Company.

Visit us at DeseretBook.com

Library of Congress Cataloging-in-Publication Data

Smurthwaite, Donald, 1951-
  The boxmaker's son / Donald S. Smurthwaite.
     p. cm.
  ISBN-10 1-59038-704-X (hardbound : alk. paper)
  ISBN-13 978-1-59038-704-7 (hardbound : alk. paper)
  1. Fathers and sons—Fiction. 2. Mormons—Fiction. 3. Portland (Or.)—Fiction. I. Title.
  PS3569.M88B69 2007
  813'.54—dc22   2006033407

Printed in the United States of America
R. R. Donnelley and Sons, Crawfordsville, IN

10 9 8 7 6 5 4 3 2 1

For a family who lived on Haig Street

CHAPTER 1

June 1959

My father was a boxmaker. That was his trade, that is what he did. He took pieces of corrugated paper and shaped them into something useful, something that we all need. His boxes were functional and not made to attract attention. No one in his working life, thirty years of it, ever told him he made a pretty box. No one, that is, until I did, on the day he made his very last box.

His job required him to rise early in the morning and to put in long hours, but he didn't mind. "Whatever it takes," he used to say—even if it meant working late at night or on Saturdays or coming in on a holiday because one of the machines had broken down. Boxes, you see, were important to him. I think he made good boxes.

In the gray, early mornings of my boyhood in Oregon, I can hear the sounds of a breaking day: The clock radio's switch tripping, the announcer's voice: "Good morning, it's five-thirty in the City of Roses, forty-seven degrees under cloudy skies, time now for the news . . ." and the sound of, first, his feet, then his knees, touching the floor. Then the creaking of his closet door opening, the sweep of his hand on hangers, the closing of the door, and his soft footsteps toward the bathroom. The hiss of the shower, the quiet rustle as he dresses. And soon, the aroma of the only breakfast I ever knew him to eat: two eggs, fried, over-easy; three strips of bacon; and one piece of toast.

By quarter after six, he is ready for his day's work. He walks softly back to his room and kisses my mother, who, by then, is stirring, and again, his footsteps—light across the old hardwood floor, followed by his opening of our front door and the soft click it makes as it closes. Then, only sounds from the world outside my home. The sputtering to life of the car's engine; the humming of the wheels moving down the street until it fades from hearing; the groan and hiss of our furnace; and because I am in Oregon, often, the gentle drumming of drizzle against my window.

My father rose earlier than any of the dads on my block and often he was the last to come home.

Yet one thing more, before the door clicks and he goes to where the boxes are made. One thing more, that I remember out of sequence, perhaps saving the best memory to recall last. Silently, between when he leaves mother and opens the front door, he peers into my room, hesitates a few seconds, looking at my brother, Tom, and me on our bunk beds. Then he walks down the hallway of our small white house and gazes into the room where my sisters sleep—Maggie, Rosie, and Claire—and for a moment watches them, too.

Looking back, I think those predawn gray visits to our rooms were like a prayer to him, a second prayer after the first, a silent petition for his children before he left. Seeing all of us, sleeping or mostly asleep, in the morning dimness that cloaked my hometown three seasons a year, a way of saying thanks, a way of asking for simple gifts—that he would come home and we would come home, and all begin again the same way tomorrow.

Prayers can be spoken, prayers can be silent, and sometimes, prayers are acted out in the way you start your day. My father prayed in all these ways.

He was, to a world that didn't know him, an average man living in an average neighborhood. The houses on my street were ordinary: most of them white, little more than a thousand square feet; sturdy brick chimneys; wide porches; and big front windows. Our street was made of an oily asphalt, speckled with embedded gravel. In the summer, when the temperatures rose, the road would turn thick and gooey, and to spare the carpet we always took our shoes off before entering the house. There were a few good trees along the block, branches thick and low-hanging, perfect for climbing. Our favorite tree was a golden delicious apple tree in the Mitchells' yard, but we never climbed it. We all waited with patience until its fruit was ready, and an air of excitement as thick as an October Oregon fog hung in our neighborhood the last few days before Mr. Mitchell stepped out of his house, picked a golden delicious, took a bite from it, and passed the word along our street: "The apples are ready. The apples are yours for the picking, kids. Just leave a few for me."

In my ordinary neighborhood, what a man did to earn a living held no status for good or otherwise. And being the son of a boxmaker wasn't anything special. You were who you were, and no one ever thought to adopt pretense. It just wasn't our way. On our block, along the black-and-oiled dead-end street, lived a retired postman, a traffic cop, a carpenter, a labor union official, a steelworker, and another man whose occupation was only known to us as "running a business." On the next block over, the dentist, Dr. Neeland, lived, the only man to graduate from college in our neighborhood, but his profession and education didn't set him apart from anyone else. As with the other men on the street, he was expected to play ball with the children, lean over the fence for good conversation with his neighbors, help paint a home or put shingles on a worn roof, and trim the hedge that grew in front of Mrs. Munson's home, the neighborhood's only widow. Dr. Neeland was different only in that, on occasion, he was asked to fill a cavity or pull a tooth at a late hour when a neighbor's discomfort became too great to bear and an appointment could not wait. No one called him Dr. Neeland, except when you were in his office, white knuckles on his chair, listening to the zizz of his drill. Otherwise, he was just Mike, one of the neighbors.

That's the way it was in that neighborhood. If you were a dentist, you helped when someone had a toothache. If you were a carpenter, you fixed the split wood in your neighbor's window casing. If you were a policeman, you occasionally let the neighborhood kids crawl into your patrol car and turn on the red flashing lights. If you were a boxmaker, you brought home a few extra boxes for your neighbors' mailings at Christmastime. And no one ever thought of asking for a nickel from anyone. That is the way our neighborhood was.

In the summer, when you put out a sprinkler on your lawn, you expected to attract a group of children. You allowed the neighbor kids to use your backyard for games of hide-and-seek and kick-the-can at twilight on summer evenings and didn't mind if they hid in your shrubbery or climbed a tree, as long as they were careful enough not to break a branch. If a baseball came through your window from one of the neighborhood games, you waited for a knock at the door or you walked outside and handed the baseball to the red-faced boy, and you didn't lecture and certainly didn't shout because that would not be neighborly. Baseballs back then cost a dollar, and were a communal purchase: nickels and dimes and pennies, pooled and held by the oldest boy in the neighborhood. A boy who chipped in a quarter became an instant hero and would start at shortstop or first base or pitcher, whatever position he wanted, when the next game began on the street in front of our homes. When a new ball was needed and enough money had been gathered for one, the whole lot of us marched to the five-and-dime store three blocks away and with soberness hefted and fingered each ball in the bin, comparing thoughts and observations with each other.

"Seams are tighter on this one."

"This one feels slick, like wax."

"This one feels too heavy."

"This one's just right. Let's get it."

Then we made the purchase, with the shiny white ball

handed from boy to boy to admire once we were out of the store.

Baseballs had a short life in our neighborhood, seldom lasting much beyond a month in the summertime. They had a hard rubber coating, which made them bounce high and go far, but we quickly wore them out, which happens when you play your games on the street. Sometimes, the ball would land in someone's yard, and it seemed as if the earth yawned and swallowed it up, never to be found again. "Lost ball!" was the cry we all dreaded the most. It meant the game would stop and we all would comb through the trees and shrubs, trying to locate our precious ball. Sometimes we found the lost ball, sometimes we didn't. And when we didn't, the pooling of our nickels and dimes and quarters began again.

All the parents understood how important the communal baseball was to us. That's why adults never lectured. They just picked up the ball when one slammed through a window or door screen and waited for the timid knock, then simply handed you back the ball. Boys and baseballs and broken windows all came in the same bundle; that was the accepted wisdom in our neighborhood, and generally thought a good thing. It kept the boys on the street—not *off* the street. On the street, where a mother or father could look out their big front window and perfectly see our world, see their boys at play. And it might be your boy who next time crushed the ball that shattered the window and dribbled in front of a neighbor's easy chair just as he sat down to watch *Bonanza* or *Wagon Train*, the sports section of the afternoon newspaper crumpled in his lap, the thoughts of his workday rapidly fading.

When the ball cracked through a window, usually within an hour or so, and never more than the day after, the offending boy's father would also knock on your door, tools in hand, and begin the repair job.

"Hello, Walter."

"Hello, Pete."

"I guess you know. My boy put a hole in your window and so I'm here to fix it, if it won't put you out any."

"Nope. Now's as good a time as any. We're just finishing dinner. Would you like a piece of cake that Ellen baked this afternoon?"

"Maybe when I'm done. First things first, and that's your window tonight. Sorry again about it."

"That won't be a problem. That boy of yours can hit it a mile. I watched him from the front window the other night. Next time, have him hit it more toward center, though."

"Will do. He feels awful bad about this."

"It's okay. My Gene hit one through your window not too long ago."

That was our life. That was my life, growing up. Simpler times, simple days, a gentle neighborliness prevailing. Granted, there was the occasional tiff between neighbors: the time when Mrs. Munson tried to pay the Tuller boy five dollars for picking up her mail while she was away visiting a daughter and Sam Tuller being sent back to her house by his father, the five-dollar bill in his hand, and a sheepish look on his face. "Dad says I should've never taken it, so here it is," he explained. "He said neighbors don't pay neighbors for things." And there was another time, when Richie Jeffers hit a ball through the Hendersons' kitchen window and Mr. Jeffers denied it was his son who had done it, even though we all saw him do it. Mr. Henderson silently replaced the broken pane and, coincidence or not, the Jefferses moved a year later.

You didn't think about who earned how much, who was getting ahead, and who was falling behind, but if someone was falling behind, you knew, without a word ever spoken about it, and you helped out in whatever quiet way you could, because worse than hard times was the loss of your pride. There were no fences in our neighborhood, no barriers or walls, but there was a finely honed sense of minding your own business. The only sin in our neighborhood was butting in and being nosy, and that almost never happened. You knew just enough about everyone else, but not any more than that.

There were times, though, when your news became the neighborhood's news, such as a family wedding, the birth of a child, a daughter going away to college, or a son going into the military. And on those occasions, it was okay to ask questions. If the news were good, then people got together and celebrated according to the nature of the event. When the Nelsons bought the first color television set on the block, a stream of neighbors came by for three days straight, slack-jawed and astonished, gawking at the rainbow screen.

The purchase of a new automobile was likewise an occasion for a neighborhood ritual. When someone bought a car, it became a spectacle for the entire block. You drove your new car home and parked it on the driveway that evening, not in the garage, even if it was raining. Soon enough, the men in the neighborhood would saunter your way, hands in pockets, eyes peering inquisitively over the tops of the thick black frames of their glasses, gathering around the new auto, sighs and approving grunts gradually evolving into conversation.

"See you got yourself a new Belair, Fred."

"Yep. We did. Got tired of driving the old Ford. It was getting up there in miles. The sales fellow made me a good deal. Got more than I thought for the Ford on trade-in."

"You going to like being a Chevy man?"

"Think so. We'll see."

"How's it do on gas?"

"Pretty good, I think. Gas is up to twenty cents a gallon now, wouldn't be surprised if it went to a quarter. Should help us out that way, especially on the summer trips. You can burn a lot of gas on a two-week vacation. Might go to Yellowstone this summer. Could add up."

"Yes, it can. Mind if I take a look under the hood? See what she's got?"

"Not a'tall."

And soon there would be four or five of the neighbors inspecting the engine, careful in their observations, poking at the spark plugs, pulling on the belts, mumbling their approval. Within minutes of the men's arrival, the mothers and children of the neighborhood would be out to admire the new car. No one ever spoke a bad word about the new car. It just wasn't done. Even when Mr. Martino bought an Edsel, all he heard was gentle praise and hopeful sentiments from the neighbors.

Those new-car evenings usually ended with the kids drinking Kool-Aid and sucking on Junior Mints provided by the owners of the new car, while the parents, couple by couple, took a spin around the block in the vehicle.

"Nice car you got there, Fred. Real nice. Might look at one like it myself, next time I'm in the market."

And at night, you would always hear your parents talking after they went to bed.

"That's a nice car. Cost a pretty penny, I bet. Fred said he got a good deal, though."

"I suppose, dear."

"You think we might be able to look at a new car? We'll hit 50,000 miles this fall. That's getting up there. Trade it in while it's still got some value. We might get a thousand for it."

"We'll see. Maybe. Maybe next year, too. Gracie needs braces."

"I suppose she does. But my crooked teeth never bothered you, did they?"

They were easy times, good times. Ike was president, the Chicago White Sox would thunder by the Yankees in the pennant race but lose to the Dodgers in the World Series, and we'd all study the black night sky for a glimpse at what the Russians called *Sputnik,* as it hurtled toward the dark side of the moon. *Ben Hur* was playing at the movie houses, Alaska and Hawaii were new states, and the Platters crooned "Smoke Gets in Your Eyes." A bad war was behind us and a shorter war seemed to end in a draw, and we were okay with that. We were only mildly concerned about a little-known soldier named Castro taking over in Cuba. It was a time for watching your television at night, wondering what Ed Sullivan would have on, and listening to the home team play ball on your table radio. You were comfortable with who you were and who your neighbors were. It was as sweet and gentle as the spring day in Oregon when the roses first bloomed and the wind drifted in from the north, which always meant fair weather ahead.

On Sundays, most of us went to church. The girls wore pastel dresses and black patent-leather shoes, the boys a white shirt and bow tie. The fathers wore solemn black suits, skinny ties, and old dark shoes, always polished. The ladies wore conservative print dresses, and they always had their hair fixed just right. On special occasions—Christmas and Easter, certainly, and when a baby was christened or there was a death in the family—the women donned prim hats.

Some attended the Lutheran Church, some went to the Methodist, most to the Catholic, and a few, to none at all. Ours was the only Latter-day Saint family in our neighborhood. While that made us a bit of a novelty, no one ever made fun of me or our family as we went to church, or of where we went to church. There was no teasing, no taunting. For the boys, more than where you went to church, how well you fielded a hot grounder or how far you could hit a ball were the measurements of your acceptance and status.

Those easy, congenial days of grace. Maybe there was more to them than I remember now; maybe, because I was small and young and not aware of nuance and hint, I didn't recognize undercurrents, didn't pick up on subtleties. But there was no need to.

I was a boxmaker's son. One boy among the bunch of an ordinary group of kids.

And yet, it was there, in that little world of my neighborhood and in my church, that the transition began, first from boyhood to something else, and then, from something else toward manhood. And from manhood to learning the certain art of making good boxes.

Even at an early age, I understood intuitively that there was more to making a good box than feeding corrugated paper into a machine.

I asked my father once if he enjoyed making boxes and he said yes. I asked him why, and he didn't give me an immediate answer. But when he came home the next day from work, he looked at me and simply said, "Because people need boxes. I want to make good boxes for them."

I suppose, too, that it was back in those days that I decided that, somehow, I wanted to become a boxmaker, too.

No description of those early years and my neighborhood would be complete without describing the churches we all attended. Much of who we all were came from deep roots in those local churches.

The Catholic Church was situated on a hill about a mile from our house. It was a long and low building with splashy stained-glass windows and a school next to it. The Lutherans and Methodists each had churches on 39th Avenue, two blocks from where I lived. They were newer buildings, two stories, each with a tall steeple and bells that rang, not by hand, but by pushing a button, or so said Jackie Crosby, whose family alternated attendance at the two churches, depending on which sermon seemed most interesting and contained a lesser quotient of guilt that week.

They were nice buildings, and all the neighbors were pleased that where we lived was home to several churches and that a simple belief in God and heaven and a sense of right and wrong was part of the fabric of our neighborhood. And it added to the overall gauzy good feeling of our neighborhood to see families, dressed in Sunday finest, all climb into their cars just before nine o'clock each Sabbath morning and drive away to their several services.

But where my family went to church was different from the others, set apart not only by theology and doctrine, but feel and distance.

Our chapel was located three miles from our home, a fact not lost upon our neighbors. "Hal, you'd save some time and money by attending one of the churches close to here," a neighbor would occasionally tease. "Must cost some gas money to get there and back, as often as you go. Why don't you come with Terri and me on Sunday? We don't bite at our church, if you're wondering." And my father, with a slight smile, would answer, "Oh, I suppose I could save a few dollars, but I'm kind of attached to where I go now, so there's no need for me to change. Besides, it's such a pretty building where I go."

And what a pretty building it was! To this day it remains a grand building, where so much of what was important to me took place. It was there, in a building of stone, wrapped in ivy, encircled by roses, where so much of my story begins and a big part of it ends.

The old church building on Harrison Street. In my memory it lives, it stands and lives, and with a touch as soft as a mother's caress, its made-in-the-mind image summons feelings as fresh as though my childhood were only days ago.

I had my neighborhood, a place of comfortable routines and predictable rhythms. And I had my church building, the very thought of which still breathes warmth and hope and life itself into me.

Can a building engender respect? Can a building, mere rock, wood, and mortar, seem a living, breathing, teaching thing? Can a building mold your experience, shape who you are, set you on a course that will carry you far away from it but not far from what you learned and felt there?

Yes, of course it can. All of those things and more. My home ward—a century old, the first building of its kind in a place of year-round, verdant green foliage and gray satin skies—provided those things for me.

Back then, you had two places of comfort as a child, your home and your church, the school house lagging far behind. Some things don't change much: for most of us, you can still have two places of comfort as an adult, your home and your church.

I see that building as clearly today as when I first became aware of it, the place we went on the Sabbath, when we dressed in different clothes and set our daily pace to a different, inner pulse.

The slate gray stone of its exterior was quarried from a river gorge nearby, thousands or millions of years or mere days in the making. The tall, opaque, leaded, stained-glass panels of the chapel windows, peaked at the top, provided a certain light to the chapel, with its rows of worn, wooden pews. The looping, circular driveway, bordered in spring and summer by rose bushes with red, pink, and yellow blooms. The high-backed red velvet chairs, where the bishopric and speakers sat, behind and above the choir. The tall pipes of the organ, their vents carved to look like open mouths of a solemn, wooden choir. And in the back of the chapel, a mural of the Good Shepherd, holding close to His breast one lamb, with others trailing behind. Beyond that wall, the huge room—wood floored and paneled, stain-glassed—called in those days the recreation hall.

"They don't make them that way anymore."

Through the years, on my infrequent trips back, when I show this place of stone, ivy, and rose to friends and family, that is the remark I hear most often. It is true: they do not build buildings like this one any longer.

When you walked up the stone stairs to that building, you always felt set apart, special. You felt there is a God in heaven and that He is aware of who you are and where you were and that you had come to this beautiful building to worship. You felt that, even as an ordinary boy growing up in an ordinary neighborhood.

Mr. Melvin Collins, history teacher, my junior year in high school. Maybe our neighbors don't care much about my family's faith, but Mr. Collins does. Mean as an ornery rattlesnake, feisty as a bandy rooster, he leans over me, sixth period, Room 114. The class is quiet. All eyes are upon Mr. Collins and on me.

"You're one of the Mormons, aren't you?"

Hesitation, then, "I am."

He looks as though he wants to say something. Something designed to do damage, to introduce doubt, to shake faith. But somehow he can't get the words out.

After a full, uncomfortable thirty seconds go by, our eyes locked, he spits out, "Well, at least your building is impressive," spins and walks away.

In times when families move every few years and we seem a people born on wheels, more than ever we need places strong because they are made of stone yet friendly enough to sprout roses on their aprons. We need places, we need neighbors and neighborhoods, and we need churches, and if some of them are old and made of stone, so much the better. When we have no place, we have no roots; when we have no roots, we all too easily can dry and shrivel and simply blow away in a hot wind.

"I like where you go to church," says one of my friends, Paul Rosa, when we couldn't have been more than five or six years old. "It's pretty. Do you see God in there?"

"Yes," I tell him. "We do."

My roots go back to that neighborhood, that church, the people I knew, my family.

"The building is beautiful. I've never seen one like it."

They say that, too, almost as often as they say it is a place no longer made. The curving lines of the windows, the tall straight lines from ground to ceiling, the steep-pitched slate roof, the grand stone stairway leading to the entrance of the building, and a thousand other features all worked in harmony and radiated a spirit of beauty and peace, matched in my experience perhaps only by some temples.

―――――

But the building is only a part of it all. Just as the houses on my street took character only because of the people who lived in them, our chapel's character was the sum of the personalities of those who attended there. Those who unlocked the doors early each Sunday, those who polished its floors on Saturdays, those who stood at the pulpit and spoke, those who sat in the pews and prayed the prayers that only Heaven could hear. They are a part of this all, too, maybe the most important part of this complicated equation that resulted, in the case most familiar to me, in preparing a boy for all that life offered and all that life would fling at me in years to come.

―――――

These people who called the building their home ward are as real to me as the edifice itself: family, friends, teachers, leaders. They are but closed eyes and a good memory away. They are those who took the time, those who understood the tap, tap, tapping of the Spirit and saw something remarkable in an unremarkable brown-eyed boy, who felt most secure within the walls of that building. I remember their names and recall their kindnesses. Many have gone on, many I will never see again, but they remain with me, and their teachings remain imprinted on my soul. They would be surprised at their influence upon me. They would be surprised that I remember their names, what they said, where they said it, and how, after decades, they still inspire. They would be surprised that they, beyond my family, taught me charity. From them to me, and in my own way, from me to others who walk hallways on Sunday, teach lessons, direct music, and place a loving arm around a shoulder.

But the building itself. Sometimes, I lie awake and think of it and imagine walking through it. I long to smell the varnish of the pews, shuttle across the parquet floor of the recreation hall, run my hand along the old velvet curtains decoratively draped to the sides of the stage. I want to feel the bubbled surface of the leaded-glass windows of the chapel, hear the clatter of dishes being washed in the kitchen after a ward social. I want to hear the ward choir, like most ward choirs, sometimes sweet and melodic, sometimes off-pitched and rumbling. I want to hear the bass anchor of Brother Caine's thunderous voice, the soaring clarity of Sister Niles's soprano, heavenly in its expression, graceful in its delivery. I want to feel Bishop Ranstrom's hand on my shoulder, hear his low, comforting voice, and see the look on his face that always conveyed I was someone with things to do in this world, a mission to complete. I want to hear Brother James as the master of ceremonies for the ward talent show, making people laugh and cry and laugh again.

They were good days. The flowers. The flowers always seemed to bloom there, even in the winter. It was easy and graceful and the pace so lovely. In my mind, I see the men of the priesthood handing a fresh flower to an elderly sister. It was as simple as snapping one from a rose bush that lined the curved driveway in the back of the building, and how often I heard words such as: "Oh, thank you, Brother Riggs. How did you know it was five years ago this week that my Howard passed away? How thoughtful of you. How kind."

Every chapel, large or small, should have a flower garden in the back, for just such reasons.

This building. Some may say it is just a structure, it is a thing only, and we cannot love things too much because things all go away. Some would say the same of your neighborhood. But your roots set the direction of your heart, and your heart sets the direction of your life.

What I am, then, comes from two places and the people I found there almost fifty years ago: one was my modest white home in a middle-class neighborhood on the southeast side of the city, where we played baseball and hide-and-seek, where we splashed in tiny vinyl wading pools and drank cold lemonade in the August heat, where we tromped in big mud puddles on the long walk home from school. The other place was the revered stone chapel on Harrison Street.

But my old neighborhood has changed, and if I walked through it, no one would recognize me, and it would not be comfortable to see others in the homes of the people I grew up with. Only the Brummels and the Martinos and the Baileys and the Mitchells, Mrs. Munson, the Tullers, and the Accardis should live in those homes. No others. But they're gone. Only the chapel still stands as my tangible link and anchor to those times.

It was my home ward, the place I grew up in. I think of the building and I think of my father, who made boxes for a living, and they seem to be the two mighty pillars as I grew up.

And it is true.

They don't make them like that anymore. Buildings or boxmakers.

The world has changed so much since then, when my father and the church building were two immovable anchors in my life. Now, few things remain constant, and there is loss in that. When you are the age I am now, you long for peace, you long for caring, you long for sweetness once found on all sides, there for the taking, in days gone by. You think of home, of longer, more innocent days.

If it were simpler, if it were sweeter. If you could hit a baseball through a window and only knock on the door and have an adult, a neighbor, hand it back to you with only the slightest of cautions: Be a little more careful out there, son. Watch out when Rudy's up. I've seen him, and he always pulls the ball to left. I'd rather not have two windows broken in one day. When your game is over, I've got some Popsicles in the refrigerator for you and the rest of the boys. C'mon by then.

C'mon by then.

Here's a quarter for you. Next time you need a new ball, use it, this quarter, to get you started. Now get along, but remember the Popsicles.

Today, if your son hits a ball through a window, you might end up in court.

The Popsicles always tasted good at the end of a baseball game, on what seemed to be those endless summer evenings.

We all have our harbors, but the very plan we supported in worlds before this dictates that we must someday sail away from them, even our neighborhood and home ward. But to go back. Someday, I'll go back, I'll go back to my street, to the church. Peaceful places have always been prominent in our collective story: Joseph in the grove, Moses on the mount, the Christian people of America and their two hundred years of Zarahemla, the Savior in His wilderness.

I want to see the building from my past, a place like stone in memory and rose in sweetness. My father is gone, as is my mother, and my siblings are scattered. But the building endures. I will find my way back. I will go back to my old street. I will go back to the old church building and see what I can see, feel what I can feel.

By long chance, maybe one of the old neighbors is still there, or maybe one of the ward members still attends church at the Harrison Boulevard building.

Maybe, boys still play baseball on the street where I grew up.

CHAPTER 2

July 1964

I am twelve years old, a Boy Scout, on a July Wednesday evening, hazy blue skies overhead. Our Scoutmaster is Brother Hutton, fair-complexioned, boyish, buoyant. He says, "Okay, boys, let's go play steal-the-flag on the side of the church," and we run to the door of the Scout room, around a corner and through another doorway that leads to the lush green lawn, presided over by Brother Newell, the building custodian and groundskeeper. "Brother Newell," my father says, "is the finest custodian in the Church. He is there all hours of the day and night and always working and everything is in tiptop shape, always. Brother Newell is the best," my father says. And I believe him. The building gleams and the grounds are immaculately groomed. Brother Newell, I hear adults say, knows every inch of the building like the back of his hand, knows every flower, knows every blade of grass.

It is the grass, in fact, that has his attention this night.

In my neighborhood, I am a little younger than one knot of boys, a little older than the next. The pecking order is set. For now, the older boys dominate in summer games of baseball.

It's a circle that I can't break into.

"Rogers, you be steady catcher."

Steady catcher, the position lowest on the rung of neighborhood baseball. Steady catcher. It meant you were the constant catcher, standing behind the batters for both teams, chasing foul balls, tossing back missed pitches or those that weren't good enough to swing at. Laboring as steady catcher was part of paying your dues. If, at the end of the game, everyone was in a pretty good mood, the steady catcher would be allowed to bat. A few pitches would be tossed his way, none of them counting toward the score. You would just take your bat up and swing hard, trying to hit the ball far, so that maybe you could turn a head or two and be included on a real team the next time a game got started.

As we tumble out of the building on that particular evening, Brother Newell stands at the edge of his manicured lawn, arms folded, stone-faced except for an unmistakable frown drooping like an inverted half-moon across his chin. *His* lawn, and a dozen boys are about to play on it, play hard, and it will not look the same when the last daring dash is made and the flag captured and a dozen sweaty boys flop on the grass, exhausted. The grass will be flat and will have lost its luster. If we fall or skid, ugly brown scars of soil may lace the lawn. Brother Newell wags a finger at my Scoutmaster, who knows the lecture and warning that await him, and walks slowly toward young Brother Hutton. The eternal question of whether boys were made for lawns or lawns were made for adults is about to be addressed and answered.

Brother Newell stands guard on the border of the lawn, hands on hips, a steady and stern gaze focused on our Scoutmaster. To his credit, Brother Hutton, twenty years Brother Newell's junior, walks purposefully toward him, his eyes locked on those of our custodian, a disarming smile spread across his features. All of the Scouts on the lawn, which had been watered earlier in the day and was still damp, pause and watch the two men. They are close enough to speak, and do so in low tones. Brother Newell's eyes dart to us, then back to Brother Hutton. He shakes his head sideways. He nods his head up and down. His expression is still solemn. Jay Hutton stands tall, runs his hands across his green Scoutmaster's shirt, turns to the side and gestures our way.

I think, *I don't know what they are saying but it seems serious and something larger than what I understand is going on. All I want to do is play steal-the-flag.*

Once, after more than an hour of being the steady catcher, the game was called, and one of the older boys said, "Let Rogers hit a couple. He's been a good steady catcher."

After some mumbling, a couple of players ambled out to shag whatever I hit, and Rusty Clement trotted out in front of the Tuller's house to lob a few pitches my way. I picked up a wood bat and walked toward home plate, marked by another player's glove. I waggled the bat with more menace than I felt and waited for Rusty's first pitch.

Kenny Getz runs and trips and slips and slides on the damp grass, and its greenness is folded into a soupy streak of brown mud.

Brother Newell folds his arms even tighter and scowls.

Brother Hutton blithely ignores the look on Brother Newell's face and shouts, "Safe at home, Kenny!"

Brother Newell turns away. Brother Hutton puts a friendly arm around his shoulder. Brother Newell stiffens and looks over his right shoulder, toward the West Hills. They talk. We choose sides for steal-the-flag. We begin our game. I make a mad dash across the grass, but I am caught and sent to prison.

Finally, Brother Newell's hands drop to his side, and he turns toward us and smiles a very tight and resigned smile and looks one last, longing time at the perfect grass on the side of the building, and his head moves up and down, slowly, up and down.

Brother Hutton also turns and we can see the full of his face for the first time since the discussion began, and he is looking pleased with himself. He starts toward us, then hesitates and turns around. He extends his hand. Roy Newell takes it and shakes it with solemnity.

Brother Hutton ambles toward us, nears us, crouches, opens his arms wide, and asks, "Whose side am I on?"

The answer, of course, is, "All of ours!"

Rusty says, "This one's coming right down the middle, Neal. Give it a ride. I'll throw it easy."

With that, he tosses the ball, and it comes in big and tantalizing and slow. I draw back my bat and swing from my heels. The ball ticks off the end of the bat, dribbles a few feet down the first-base side, and stops.

"Good cut, Neal. Try again."

His second pitch floats in. I cock my bat and swing with all my might. The result is almost the same. A limp foul ball that goes nowhere, the same approximate destination as my neighborhood baseball status.

"One more."

Before we begin, Brother Hutton calls us together and says, "Okay, fellows. Here's what it is. Brother Newell says we can play on the grass tonight. But he asks us not to be reckless and not slide on the grass if we can help it. Brother Newell works hard and we need to respect what he does for us. But we can play. He said it's okay for us to do that."

Later in the evening, when we were spent and tired and sweaty, when our jeans were stained grass-green, and we had experienced a wonderful hour of playing steal-the-flag, I flopped on the ground not far from Brother Hutton. He stood with his hands on his hips, pleased in the knowledge that he, an adult, still had something in reserve, while his dozen Scouts were simply out of gas.

The last pitch comes in, nice, easy, belt high. Rusty is doing me a favor.

I tense, draw back the bat, and swing as hard as I can.

I miss the ball.

Three strikes.

"Good cut, Neal," Rusty has the decency to say. *Good cut* is what they always say when you have failed miserably, as I have. I am doomed to be the steady catcher for weeks ahead. Discouraged, I reach for my own glove and scuff toward my house.

A brother in the ward came up to Brother Hutton and asked, "How did you get Roy to let the boys play on that lawn? You know how he feels about it. Guards it like he would if someone were threatening his own children. Roy's a good man, but stubborn when it comes to his lawn."

Brother Hutton said, "Oh, we had a little talk all right. I told him a story that I heard once. About boys and a yard and the punch line to it all was something like, 'The grass will come back. But will the boys?'

"Roy is the father of three boys. Only two have come back. I guess that's all there was to it. A little grass isn't much of a price to pay, is it? For your boys to come back? To keep your boys here?"

The other adult nodded and the great question was answered.

Lawns were made for boys.

My father was watering our grass when I got home, directing a fine stream of spray rhythmically across our yard. He glanced at me when I approached and gave a knowing look.

"I saw you out there, taking those swings," he said. "Good cuts."

"I didn't hit it."

"I know. You were trying too hard. What do you think?"

"I dunno."

"When you get two strikes on you next time, choke up on the bat. Move your hands a little higher on the barrel. Don't try to kill it. Just make contact. Pretend the ball is a bumblebee and you're going to swat it. You'll be surprised at how far the ball will go."

"I'll try. Okay. I don't know. Okay."

"It's a good rule. For baseball," he said, and then turning to water another patch of lawn, he said something like, "and for life."

Brother Hutton would someday be Bishop Hutton, and he would be the one who conducted the sacrament meeting when I left on my mission and when I returned and reported back. At my, what we used to call, "missionary farewell," he would talk about that evening on the grass, Brother Newell's lawn, and how it was on that evening, he first noticed something that caused me to stand out. He said he'd noticed I tried extra hard not to slide on the grass, not to leave a brown smear where the lawn grew. He said it was then he knew that I knew what it meant to respect others. He said he could tell that I was

Hal Rogers's son. He said he thought I would be a good missionary, because I didn't slide on the lawn.

In my yard, in the summer afternoon, I pick up a bat and move my hands up on its barrel. I take a few swings, then a few swings more. I want to feel comfortable the next time I get two strikes and need to choke up.

My father watched all of this play out from the street along the west side of the church. He stood there, next to his two-tone Oldsmobile, blue-on-the-bottom, white on top, big fins flaring from the rear of the car, little round tail lights at the top of the fins. He stood there in his working clothes: beige cotton pants, beige short-sleeved shirt, blue canvas shoes. He had come to pick me up from Scouts. He had come straight from work, where he had stayed late, making his boxes.

I don't know when I got to bat again. Probably a couple of weeks later. In the meantime, I stationed myself behind the batter and played steady catcher in the neighborhood games and dreamed about the next time I would get a chance to bat. It happened the same way, at the end of a game. This time, Sam Tuller took over as pitcher, and a couple of the other boys lazily ran a few dozen yards behind him. Keep the kid humored. Let him take a few swings. No big deal. We need a steady catcher, so that one of us doesn't have to.

I picked up a bat and stood facing Sam. I moved my hands

higher on its barrel. I waited for the first pitch. It came, a lob, easy to hit. I didn't swing, as I had before, with all my might. I just tried to hit it.

I remember the sound—a thwack—and the sweet sensation of the ball jumping off the bat. I remember the low arc of the ball and watching it skitter between the two boys playing in the outfield. I remember Sam looking at me, perhaps with respect, definitely with surprise.

"Good hit, Neal. Good hit."

He pitched a half dozen more to me, with close to the same results each time I swung. The other boys standing around stopped what they were doing and watched me hit.

I found out something that day. I was not meant to be power hitter, a slugger. I was meant to hit line drives. I was a better player when I choked up on the bat.

"Saw you out playing ball a little," Dad said. "How did it go out there for you today?"

"Better. Got a few good hits."

"So I noticed."

I never had to play steady catcher again.

We played steal-the-flag dozens of times more on that great green slope, and I hope that boys play there to this day.

Something more about this mixture of lawns and boys and fathers, and keeping the grass green.

Brother Newell occasionally came out to watch us.

Once, he even joined in.

He ran faster than any of us thought a man his age could. And when it was over, he flopped on the lawn and laughed with us, and plucked handfuls of grass and playfully threw them into our hair.

Lawns were made for boys.

Lawns were made for Brother Newell.

CHAPTER 3

September 1964

My father and I were home teaching companions for five years, from just before I turned fourteen to the time I left for my first year in college.

Five years, and during that time, we home taught a grand total of one active family. All the others were less fully committed.

I can see my father arriving home from the box plant on an overcast Tuesday evening. We eat dinner and then he says, "I think we'll go home teaching tonight. Is that all right with you, Neal?"

Father rarely dressed in a suit or tie to do his home teaching. Sometimes he changed his shirt, but mostly, we just went as we were. He never prepared a formal message, but he always went to a house with a plan. He rarely went into a home with his scriptures, but he knew exactly what to say.

"We'll go to the McGuires and the Rowans tonight," he would say. "We'll get the others next week."

And so we went, parking in front of an older, two-story house on Clinton Street. Up the stairs to Ned McGuire's house. A knock on the door. And then I would watch and listen as my father worked his magic.

"Fast routes, guys," Brother Hutton says, early on a Sunday morning before priesthood meeting. "There's about six envelopes in each route. Some of these you can walk to, and some you'll need to have your dad drive you to, or maybe you can ride your bike. Here we go, brethren. Turn them in at the bishop's office when you're done, before sacrament meeting tonight. Route one—Neal, you're the youngest deacon and this is the closest route. Let's assign you to this one. You can walk it between priesthood and Sunday School."

He hands me the bundle of worn brown cardboard envelopes, with the strings tied in a circle-eight pattern on the back. The name on the top of the first envelope is "Louis and Lois Broadstreet," with their address printed neatly beneath.

I say, "Who are the Broadstreets? I've never heard of them."

Brother Hutton says, "I don't know who they are. Let's see. They live just across the street. Knock on the door and tell them you're from the Church and that you are there to gather the fast offerings to help the poor and needy. That should about do it. Broadstreet," he says, puzzled. "They might not even know they're members of the Church."

And with no further instruction, the door to our class-room opens, and my quorum members and I shuffle out the door to begin our priesthood errands.

Father peers through the screen door. Inside, a man about his age stares into the flickering television set. Father calls his name.

"Hello, Ned. It's Hal. Mind if we step in?"

"Not a'tall, Hal. You and the boy are always welcome here."

"The yard's looking nice, Ned. You fertilize it? You must have. Sure is green."

"I did. A month ago. Used this stuff from Alaska. Made out of fish, and it sure smells to heaven and back for a week or so, but the grass turns deep green and fills in real nice. Don't burn the lawn, neither."

"You don't say. Fish fertilizer. Who would've guessed."

"Yep. From fish. Imagine that."

"I wouldn't of thought that."

"But it is natural. No chemicals, so, like I say, you can't burn it, and when the kids play on it, you don't worry. Except their clothes smell a bit when they come in and they might need to take a bath."

"I bet they do. But it works, that's for sure. Your lawn is beautiful."

I walk slowly away from the church, across the parking lot, and gradually make my way toward the Broadstreet home. I am uncertain of my mission and try to remember Brother Hutton's instructions. Knock. Tell them who you are. What you are here for. Listen to what they say.

My knock is timid, and I hope, in the grand tradition of fearful priesthood bearers through the ages, that no one is at home. But I hear the sound of light footsteps sweeping toward the door. It opens. A lady in her sixties, short and round, dressed in a bathrobe, spies me, smiles, and invites me in. *What now? What do I say? What did Brother Hutton tell me to say?* My mind sputters and fizzles, and I feel like a small boy.

She says, "Hello."

I look around the house. I see her gangly, balding husband sitting relaxed in a large, comfortable chair, all skinny arms and legs, reading the newspaper. I smell what is being prepared for breakfast—toast, slightly burned; the woodsy sweet aroma of frying bacon; the pungent odor of coffee.

I think, *He was right. Brother Hutton was right. These people don't know they are members, or they don't care, or something.*

She looks at me curiously. My mind comes back to life. These people may not know they are Mormons, but neither will they tie me up and keep me prisoner here. I remember what I am supposed to say.

"My name is Neal Rogers. I am from the Church. I am here to gather fast offerings to feed people who are needy and hungry. That's why I am here." I pause and glance through the open door at her yard. "Your grass is sure green. Do you use fish fertilizer on it?"

She looks at me, and I see clear eyes, clear and very blue eyes, a depth and color I have never seen before. There is fineness and a wisdom and an understanding in those eyes. On the wall is a photograph, obviously taken years before, of the

Broadstreet family—the parents and two young sons, and I think, *She is a mother, a mother of boys.*

She says, "I don't know for sure what Mr. Broadstreet uses, but he does put something on it every spring. The hungry and needy, you say? A very fine cause, Neal. Let me see. What have you in the envelope? Something for me to fill out?"

I hand her the envelope, and she looks inside of it then disappears into another room. She returns a minute later and bends down slightly and looks at me, eye to eye. I am fixed on the clarity of her eyes. I have never noticed the clear eyes of an older woman before. It is a first for me on this errand, the recognition of clarity that age brings.

"There's a little something in there. We do," she says slowly, "need to feed people who are hungry. You come back anytime, honey."

I manage a croaky "Thank you."

She says, "My name is Lois and this is my husband Louis."

On cue, Louis Broadstreet lowers his newspaper and nods at me and says in what I can only describe as a stringy voice, "Nice to meet you, sonny."

Lois Broadstreet stands to her full height, which isn't much of a height at all. She brushes something off her robe and then laughs, just laughs.

"Things going well for you, Ned?"

"Oh, yeah, Hal. Just fine. Can't complain. No one listens anyway when you do."

"That's for sure."

"How're things at the box plant?"

"Good. You know this is when we start getting busy. Most people don't think of it, but we put out a lot of boxes now so they'll be ready for the holidays."

"You've got to work ahead."

"Yes, we do. Always got to keep one eye ahead. I reckon that's good advice for more than just work."

"Funny names we have, Louis and Lois. When we first met, people said, 'Oh, you have to date and fall in love and get married. Think of the fun you'll have with names like that.' And you know what? Those people were right. We've had such fun through the years. Raised two boys, we did. You remind me of our younger son, Neal. He's a dentist, lives in Arizona. We visit him occasionally."

Her eyes, they seem to shine, they seem to have light spilling from them. Her eyes, her eyes, her dark blue eyes, they seem to see everything.

Louis Broadstreet glances up over the edge of his paper and says, "Yup. We have. Might too hot in Arizona, though. We like it here best."

"Mr. Broadstreet is from New England. He doesn't say much."

Louis Broadstreet places the newspaper in his lap and says, "Nope. Don't have to. Mrs. Broadstreet does most of the talking."

"But you come back again. We'll always put something in your envelope. We always will."

I say, "Thanks. Thanks very much." And then, trying to be

mature beyond what I am, I add, "It has been a pleasure to be in your home."

"The pleasure has been ours. And remember this, just remember," Lois Broadstreet says. "Wisdom comes often in the places you least expect it."

Louis Broadstreet, face hid behind the financial page, says, "Yup. She's right."

They made a promise that day, the Broadstreets. And they kept their word. There was something comfortable and genuine and real about them, something playful in their nature, something unspoken but good in the way they treated each other. I went to their house as often as possible on the first Sunday of each month. It was probably as close to unrighteous dominion as I've ever been—quickly grabbing the bundle of fast offering envelopes that included theirs.

I didn't realize it until later, but I had grown to love this friendly, quirky couple, and especially the woman with eyes the color of a mid-summer morning sky.

———

"Well, Neal and I need to be pushing on, Ned. You tell Lucy hello for us. Oh, and by the way, Neal here is with the Church Scout group and they're going up the Clackamas for an overnighter. If your boy wants to come along, I know Neal would watch out for him."

"We'll talk it over. Maybe Stanley would like that. We'll see and let you know."

"G'night, Ned."

"G'night, Hal, Neal."

"Take care. You take care of this family of yours."

"Sure enough. I will. You take care, too. That Neal, he's a mighty fine boy, Hal."

"You never eat. We always invite you to eat with us. It's breakfast time, Neal."

"No, thanks, Mrs. Broadstreet."

"The muffins are fresh."

"Well, no, I can't. Not today."

Louis Broadstreet walks toward me. "They're mighty good, Neal. Ought to try one. Ought to."

"I can't. Not today."

"Have it your way, then, Neal." Lois Broadstreet walks away from me and returns in a moment with the envelope. "For the poor and needy." Her blue eyes. I could never get over how blue her eyes were.

"Thank you. I'll see you next month."

And on the way back to the car, my father says, "Ned's a good man. Good family. We'll get him someday, Neal. We will. He's a good friend."

Father says, "You can tell a lot about a fellow by how he keeps his yard and if he keeps his shoes shined. Just something I picked up over the years."

Ned McGuire's yard always looked good, and his shoes were always shined.

I went to the Broadstreet home for the two years I was a deacon, and then two more when I was a teacher, because our quorums were small and we didn't have enough deacons to cover all the routes.

Lois Broadstreet always said a little saying to me before I left. Always.

"You are the one who controls your happiness."

"You will never regret acting on a good impulse. You will often regret not acting on one."

"When you marry, Neal, look for a girl who knows how to be content."

Her homilies. Sometimes corny, sometimes wise, sometimes with a bit of grit and vinegar, sometimes I just didn't understand them. But each was delivered with care and thought and, as I look back on it now, were her way of preparing and protecting me from a world that too often didn't act with care and thought.

Maybe that's the way it is with those you care for. You heap upon them all you can, all that you hope will protect them. And when the time comes when the world tears away at who you are and what you are and how you want to be, maybe you hope that you have heaped enough layers, layers of care and layers of love, to keep those you love insulated from the craziness that goes on in the world. That's what you hope for. That's how you protect those close to you. Or at least, that's how you try.

Looking back, I suppose she and her husband loved me. I suppose I really did remind them of their youngest son, the one who was a dentist in Arizona. It didn't occur to me, not at that time, that a genuine love could develop among people who just happen to meet and happen to care.

In front of the Broadstreet home one day on the way from a visit, the wind blows little raindrops against my cheek. They could be tears. Tears from a blue sky.

Stanley McGuire cocks his bat, lunges at a fastball, swings from his heels, and misses.

"Strike three!" bellows the umpire, and Stanley walks toward his dugout, bearing the weight that only a boy who has just struck out can feel and understand.

"It was a good cut, Ned. He's got potential. Now Neal here, he's a fine ballplayer, too. You send Stanley over some time and they can play catch. Neal's a little older than Stanley, so maybe he can give him some pointers. What do you say?"

"That 'ud be nice. Stanley thinks the world of Neal. Neal's a nice boy, real nice."

We would be the McGuires' home teachers for four years. During our visits, Father never wore a tie. He didn't mention the Church very often. He never taught a lesson. But he always left a message.

A while ago, a year or two back, I rummaged through a small dusty box I found in a corner of my basement. Inside, in the slanted scrawl of a boy, I found more of Lois Broadstreet's messages to me, things I heard her say in my visits to her home.

Always pay attention to people.

Never wish away time.

It's better to be kind than smart.
Time does go by faster as you age.

"You know, Hal, I've got that surgery coming up, and it isn't a big thing, well, shouldn't be a big thing anyway, but I was wondering. I think you can give me a blessing, if that's what you call it. Can't hurt me. Lucy's a little worried, you know. That's all. Stanley, he knows something's going on, too, and I don't want to worry my boy at all. So it might help. Just tell me what I need to do and I'll do it. I'm not religious, but this whole thing has me thinking."

My father says, "I'll come over on Sunday and help you out, Ned. I'll give you a blessing, that's what we call it. And I'll explain it a little to you so you'll know what will take place. It's pretty simple and about all you have to do is sit on a chair."

"Thanks, Hal. It can't hurt. Nope, it can't hurt a thing to ask."

Time and kindness were two of her recurring themes. Lois Broadstreet seemed to think a lot about both topics. She once told me, "Kindness lives on. Kindness is real and physical and it lives on and it is somewhere in the universe and it exists. It lives. It goes on. It is tangible."

I think she was right.

"So the surgery went fine, Lucy? It did? Well, that's wonderful news. I'll give Ned a day or two and then I'll run up to the hospital and visit him. I bet you'll sleep well tonight. Great news, yes, just great. We're real happy for you. It's a relief to Neal and me, too, you bet."

———

"Tell us why you don't eat with us when you visit," Lois Broadstreet asks.

I am a teacher now, more certain of myself in some ways, and I answer, "We fast two meals and use the money we would have spent on the food to care for the poor and needy."

She stops and looks upward and seems to think hard. "How profound. How profound and simple," Lois Broadstreet says. "It all equals out that way."

"Yup. Both of those," Louis adds. "Profound and simple."

"I remember that church you come from," she says. "I was baptized there, a long time ago, but I never understood much. I've not come back to it at all. Someday. Someday, maybe."

That night, I add to my prayers an appeal that she will come back indeed, and bring Louis with her, too. My prayer was simple, and, I hope, my prayer was profound.

———

My father leans a little over the small desk where our telephone perches.

"Why, that would be wonderful, Ned. You'll find a lot of nice people there. . . . Oh, no, we didn't do anything for you that anyone else wouldn't have. . . . What's a friend for? . . . See you on Sunday. I'll be at the door waiting for you."

He exchanges a little more conversation and then hangs up the receiver and sits down in his big chair and doesn't say a word. I glance over from our dinner table, where I am working on a report titled "The Fir Trees of Oregon" for science class and see just a glimmer of a smile on his face.

At home one evening, we talk about the Broadstreets. Dad and I have been asked to serve as their home teachers. My father says, "I get more out of home teaching them than I give back. Fine, fine people, the Broadstreets. Louis, I sometimes think he might have marched right off the *Mayflower*. Puritan stock, I'd guess."

Louis is retired, but he worked for more than thirty years, in a plant that made paper. And he and my father have much in common. They are friends, too.

We're in my backyard. "When you get two strikes on you, Stanley, you choke up on the bat. It gives you better control. You have a better chance of hitting the next pitch. That's it, Stanley, choke up. Hands a little higher. Okay, here comes the pitch. Ready? Nice, nice. That went a long way."

Her eyes were blue. The bluest eyes I've ever seen, a color I have never seen again.

If you need to take a pill, have enough water on hand for two.

True friendship often requires true sacrifice.

People who plot against you will only succeed if you allow them.

If a girl is the right one for you to marry, you'll never need to wonder. "You'll know. You'll just know, Neal. Mr. Broadstreet can tell you that."

So it went with the Broadstreet family. On the first Sunday of every month, I was in their home for five minutes. At least once before the end of the month, Father and I were in their home for fifteen minutes. On the surface, that doesn't seem much, certainly not enough to help steer a lifetime, but our courses are set by small degrees. And Lois's bits of advice, some wise, some almost childish, all delivered with tenderness and sweetness. I began writing down those short sermons about a year after I met the Broadstreets. I have them to this day. I need layers still.

You will go as far as your dreams will take you.
Look back with humility, look forward with hope.
Time can separate and time can unite.

Five men standing in a circle, one man sitting on a chair. Just before the circle closes in and hands are laid upon his head, the man on the chair looks the slightest bit sheepish. On the other side of the bishop's office, Lucy smiles and Stanley's eyes dart about the room, trying to absorb all that is taking place. My father begins speaking, his voice deep and serious and prayerful.

I recall the last time I was in the Broadstreets' neighborhood. On a cool, drizzly night, I walked slowly until I was in front of the house where they no longer lived. It had been updated: the new paint color, the professional landscaping, a late-model sports car in the driveway. I wish, I wish . . . that Louis and Lois were still inside, that the house were as plain and straightforward and stark as when the Broadstreets lived there. White house, blue shutters, and blue trim.

A blue to match Lois Broadstreet's eyes. How Louis must have loved those eyes. How he must have loved to drive up to his home and see the blue shutters welcoming him, a constant reminder of the woman he loved.

Blue shutters, blue eyes. The square, tidy house, like a box. The square, tidy lives of the people within those plain white walls.

My father in the parking lot of the church. "Not at all," he says. "I've done nothing special. I didn't know how nicely things would turn out," he says to Ned McGuire, "but I'm glad they have." He cocks his head heavenward. "But you have to believe, Ned, had you never stepped inside a church, you would still be my friend, and I would still come to see you and Lucy and Stanley. You have to believe that I love your family. You must believe that."

Ned McGuire looks serious and says, "Yes," he does believe it.

As we drive away, my father says, "I like people who try hard."

I long to see them. I long for what they represented—a good, simple, and kind life. In the ocean of turmoil I some-times find myself in, I long for what they represent and a cordiality that has slipped away from us, as a society and, too often, as a people. A simple life, yes, but to use one of Lois's own words, a *profound* life. The *simple* and the *profound.* There is a link, there is a link.

"Lois isn't here today. She isn't feeling well," Louis Broadstreet said one fast Sunday. I was a priest, but still often helped with the fast offering. He spoke slowly. "She knew you would come by, though. She wrote a check for the poor and needy." He turned and walked heavily toward the kitchen. He slipped the check into the fast offering envelope, and in his spare New England accent, said, "She said you'd come and to have the check ready. She said she needed to do her part and didn't want to disappoint you. Thank ye, Neal. Thank ye. You know, she, well, she . . ." and then the man of few words said nothing more.

For a lifetime, I have wondered what Louis wanted to say. I have wondered how he wanted to finish that sentence. I never saw their son from Arizona in their home. I never heard them talking about how he would be coming home. He didn't come home. That's what. He didn't. And I think Louis was going to say, "You know, she loves you, Neal. She really does."

That's what I think.

"If she isn't feeling well, we have a way to give her a blessing. It's a blessing for her health," I say. "It can't hurt. It can't."

"Thanks, son. I'll talk with her about it."

The McGuires were one among many. I see their faces, the front porches of their homes, their eyes, and this man and his boy approach for the first time. I see their suspicion, I sense their doubt. I feel a slight tension in the air. Then I listen.

"Hello, I'm Hal Rogers and this is my boy, Neal. We just wanted to drop by and say hello. Been a good day, hasn't it? Say, sure is a nice lawn you got there. You must fertilize it in the spring. My yard isn't looking so good. Tell me, what is it you use? If you wouldn't mind."

He hardly ever wore a tie when he home taught. He never had a message. He always left with a friend behind.

And his shoes were always shined.

It didn't dawn on me. It didn't register. I would come back next fast Sunday, and Lois would be there and she would talk to me and tell me something to make my world better, and I would take the check back to help feed the poor and needy. I would see those blue eyes and listen to her words and come away a better person, because, in my own case, Lois was feeding the needy in a particular way. That's what would happen, because that is what always had happened before, and at my age, your life doesn't change much, maybe not at all.

I turned to the door. Louis cleared his throat, and his words came thick and heavy.

"Ahem. She, the wife, wanted me to tell you something. She wanted me to tell you that we all rely on the extraordinary kindness of others. Her very words, they are. And she wanted me to tell you that you have been a very kind young man, son."

I said thank you, with an uneasy feeling that I had heard a prayer, not a conversation, and I didn't quite understand it, and I walked toward the street, an overwhelming sadness trailing me. At the curb, I stopped and turned and looked back at the blue shutters, the eyes of that home, and saw Louis Broadstreet gently lift his hand in a forlorn wave good-bye.

They taught me so much. And now, I must remember there are still people like the Broadstreets—they are everywhere, and their capacity to give and teach and love and add layers that protect represents a world without end. To think otherwise is to lose memory of their goodness. And goodness such as theirs deserves to be remembered, always.

The deep thick night is shattered by a phone call. In the black of my room, I hear my father's groggy voice. It is a few minutes after three a.m.

"Oh. Oh, of course. Yes, I have the consecrated oil. I'll be there right away. Thanks for calling."

Two Sundays later, Bishop Ranstrom stood in front of the congregation to conduct sacrament meeting. I remember the moment as though it were yesterday, the rustle in the congregation as the last people to the chapel were seated, the soft whimpering of a baby to my left, the way Sister Markham, our ward organist, stopped playing the prelude music, folded her hands on her lap, and watched Bishop Ranstrom, whose face was straight and lined and filled with a longing for something that had come and passed and could not be retrieved.

"I regret to tell the members of our congregation about the passing of one of our ward members, Sister Lois Broadstreet. Sister Broadstreet had been ill for quite some time. Not many of you knew her. She lived in the little home with blue shutters across the street from here."

Something inside me quivers and shakes, and I feel dizzy and heartsick. I am seventeen years old, strong as stone, yet I feel a darkness closing over me. I feel . . . I feel . . . I feel as though I had in some way disappointed the Broadstreets, let them down, not been the friend I should have. I close my eyes. I knew her. I knew her. I knew how good she was.

My father places a hand on my arm. He knew her, too. A voice from a thousand miles away says, "I'm sorry, son. I am sorry for you and for the family. I know she was your friend. She was our friend. She passed away early this morning. I should have told you."

Bishop Ranstrom speaks again. "But those of you who were acquainted know how lovely and gracious a soul she was. We will miss Sister Broadstreet. Her services will be here on Tuesday morning at eleven o'clock."

The voice of my father, only a little closer: "We'll go, Neal. We'll go together, son."

A thought comes to me. A thought from somewhere else. Maybe the thought comes to me as the voice of Lois Broadstreet: Kindness lives. It is real and tangible and it lives somewhere and will always be there. Kindness and love is matter and cannot be destroyed, but can be recalled and found over and over again. It's out there. It lives.

Otherwise, there would be no Atonement.

It is her last lesson to me, and her first, and I needed to hear it then and remember it now.

I visited Louis Broadstreet off and on for the next few years. I said good-bye to him the night before I left for college, stopped by with a small book at Christmas, and then drifted away from his life. By the time I returned home from my mission, Louis had moved. I suspect that the little Cape Cod house was too different without his beloved Lois, different beyond what he could bear. I imagine he saw her eyes each time he saw the house. The eyes of the house were there, but there were no eyes behind it.

Maybe he went to Arizona to live near his son—crisp New England salt air mixed with saguaro and ocotillo. I hope he lived well.

If I were to ever go back to that old neighborhood, ever to walk up the street where they lived, would it serve a purpose for me to knock on the door of the home and try to explain to the current residents about the people who lived there almost thirty-five years ago? If I were to do so, perhaps the residents would listen politely. Maybe they would even be interested in the history of the home where they now reside. I might even receive an invitation to come in, sit down, and tell a good story to these strangers.

But how could I tell them about the color of Lois Broadstreets' eyes, and how the shutters made me think of those eyes whenever I saw them? How would I, without sounding foolish or strange, tell them that Louis made the shutters and painted them a certain color to remind him of his wife's eyes?

I would try to tell them and hope they would understand, and if they didn't understand, I would hope they would be gracious enough to listen and nod and pretend.

And maybe I would compliment them on the vigor of their lawn and ask what kind of fertilizer they used. I might ask them if they ever heard of fish fertilizer and then just see where the conversation would go. Yes, just see where the conversation would go.

Kindness lives. It breathes and moves and is tangible, and it never goes away, and we can draw on it and also give it away as often as we need to. It was a simple lesson, and profound.

The Broadstreets taught me that.

CHAPTER 4

July 1962

My father was an ordinary man. He was of average height, average build, maybe a few pounds too heavy. He wore glasses, dark plastic rims, thick lenses. He was broad through the shoulders, and his upper arms were thick, perhaps because his work often required him to lift things. He spoke in a glassy baritone. His eyes were pale blue, his hair brown and combed straight back. His walk was smooth, suggesting a natural grace.

My home was average. It was the only home I knew until I left for college. Seven of us dwelled there: my parents, two older sisters, me, a younger brother, and our youngest sister. A small home, built mostly by my father. Three bedrooms, one bathroom, and a basement that never was finished. We lived in close quarters. Sunday mornings, use of the sole bathroom was strictly scheduled, fifteen minutes at a time, no excuses. Little wonder my sisters wore the barest of makeup, the simplest of clothing, all three, unadorned beauties. There was no time for anything more elaborate. We were plain people, living in a plain house.

Father, war-weary after four years in the South Pacific, came back to Oregon, married the girl he'd left behind, built a home, built a life. He worked for a company that made boxes, tens of thousands of them each week. He worked hard. After the South Pacific, all he wanted was never to go to war again. As a boy, I often heard him pray that wish. When those who had never fought spoke of the glories of war, he said nothing, but simply turned his head away, his shoulders slumped, and he left. It didn't matter where he was, he just left.

I stand in Creston Park and tap my baseball glove, deep in center field, while Brother Newman winds up and pitches a softball to Brother Maple, who punches a little pop-up in the air. Our first baseman waves his hands and sings to the rhythm of a ballgame, "I got it, I got it, I got it!" and the spinning ball snuggles in his glove. Three outs. We're up. Last at-bats. Tie game.

It is the ward's Pioneer Day celebration. The picnic is done—the fried chicken, baked beans, potato salad, syrupy sweet punch, Jell-O desserts all long gone. The program is over—the reenactment of Brigham Young entering the valley completed, my younger brother Tom, deep in drama, portraying the prophet, his construction-paper beard held nicely in place by masking tape. The Primary girls in their long, cotton pioneer dresses; the boys in their cowboy or Davy Crockett hats pulling Radio Flyers outfitted to look like covered wagons, toy rifles held at their sides.

What I looked forward to, what I dreamed about for nights ahead of the event, was the ward softball game among the fathers and sons, the pinnacle of the celebration for boys like me. For years, I sat on the blankets with the other children and mothers and watched the game and ached for the time when I might play, the time I could show them what I can do. The rule was ten. Ten years old and you could play. I turned ten in April. My day had come.

I will show them all what I can do.

———

Seven years and three children later, he was called back to duty, this time in Korea, leaving behind an unpainted house and a wife expecting another child in three months. The neighbors pitched in and finished painting the house—Henry Brummels, seventy years and more, with a bucket of paint on a stepladder, carefully swishing his brush across the trim of our home. The unborn baby became the sole work of my mother, who, one December night, calmly called a distant cousin who lived across town and apologetically asked for a ride to the hospital, her voice as placid as a still pond on a cool fall morning. Once there, she did the rest, and my brother was born. Father first glimpsed him almost two years later.

At the back of the parking lot now, I can see us, see us as we were then, on a typical Sabbath: the Oldsmobile station wagon pulling up, and my mother and sisters climbing out and dutifully walking up the covered backstairs that led to the side door of the chapel. The boys, except when we were too young to walk, stayed with Father, while he parked the car, then we walked up the same stairway and looked to see where Mother and the girls had settled.

Seven people, three bedrooms, one bathroom. And we were never late for church. Never.

Bishop Ranstrom had taken all of the speculation out of choosing the teams. "Everyone west of the chapel on one team, everyone east on the other. West bats first." And off I ran to play center field, like Mays and Mantle, hoping to get there before anyone else, never to be uprooted. I hoped people would notice. *See that Neal Rogers out there? He's so young. Just a little fellow. But look at the way he moves, doesn't miss a thing. Some ballplayer he'll be. Looks like he owns center field.*

And now, ninety minutes later, the game had come down to our final at-bat. Bishop Ranstrom had said, "If it's a tie, it's a tie. It's getting dark, and the sisters want to go home and the little kids are getting cranky, so this is it, brethren."

He was our bishop. No one argued. He was also the game's umpire, a fitting, though not necessarily easier, calling than being a common judge in Israel.

Our first two batters meekly grounded out and it looked as though the game would end in a tie. I was the batter, and with every ounce of determination I could muster, I silently vowed that Neal Rogers would not be the last batter in the game.

Brother Romo, the pitcher, took an exaggerated wind-up and lobbed the ball toward me, tantalizing, big as a melon, and, I thought, a little outside.

"Ball one," droned Bishop Ranstrom. "Good eye, Neal."

Players on my team echoed the chatter. Good eye, Neal. Way to look. Make him pitch to you. Hum, baby.

Brother Romo frowned. "Caught the outside corner, Bishop."

"No, it didn't. Don't argue. I'll make you the ward Scoutmaster," Bishop Ranstrom called back genially.

"I think you're right. It was a ball," Brother Romo answered playfully.

Brother Romo lofted a second pitch my way. It looked good—big and slow and easy. This was my moment. I cocked the bat, swung from my heels, heard a pleasant "thwack!" and watched a hard ground ball skip between the shortstop and third baseman. Jubilantly, I sprinted to first base. A prayer had been answered. Not a big prayer, unless you were a ten-year-old boy in his first fathers-and-sons softball game, in which case, it was a very big prayer. I happily stood on first base, hands on hips.

I would not be the one to make the final out.

My father made cardboard boxes for more than thirty years. He dressed the same way every day. Beige pants. Beige shirt. Blue canvas shoes with rubber soles, comfortable, he always said, the better to be on your feet all day.

Our Sunday shoes were always shined. Sometimes they had holes in them, but they were shined and our white shirts pressed. The girls were always in neat, clean dresses. And we were never late for church.

For Mother and Father, it would have been dishonorable to be late for church.

My father cheered the loudest for me. Perhaps that was his mistake. From behind home plate, Bishop Ranstrom looked toward him and said, "Hal, you haven't played yet. With your son on first, why don't you bat now? It is a fathers-and-sons game, you know. Boys and their dads. That'ud include you."

"Oh, I can't, Bishop. It's been years. I'd only embarrass myself."

"It's just a game. No one will remember it. Your boy is on first. Come on up, Hal."

"I don't think so, Bishop. Just don't think I have it anymore."

"You still do, Hal. Come on up and show us. Show that runner on first base."

My father looked at our bishop, then he looked at me, and he said, "You know that's not fair and not nice, Bishop, bringing my boy into it." He slowly got off the blanket he shared with Mother and Tom and walked toward our bench. He looked carefully at the bats, hefting them, and then settling on an old green wood bat, he took a tentative stance in the batter's box, adjusted his glasses, and awaited Brother Romo's first pitch. He said something to the bishop that I couldn't quite hear, but I think it was, "This better work."

At first base, I had mixed feelings of the highest order. While I had not wanted to make the final out, I did not intend to pass that dubious honor to my father. Our good family name was at stake, to my thinking. Father could make boxes, but could he hit a softball?

Brother Romo floated a pitch.

"Well, Hal, I'm going to have to call that one a strike. A little inside, but it caught the plate. So that's it," Bishop Ranstrom said. "There you go. Strike one."

Father glanced back at our bishop, grinning. "Bear down, Blue. Need to borrow my glasses?"

Brother Romo wound up and tossed the second pitch.

"That one missed, Gary. A little low, I think," Bishop Ranstrom announced his judgment. "Ball one. Even count at one. Let's get moving, fellas. It's almost dark."

Brother Romo pretended to be angry and kicked some dust and stomped around on the pitcher's mound. My father stepped away from the batter's box and pushed his glasses higher on his nose. He took a practice swing, then back in the box, he dug his heels into the dust. At first base, I fretted and worried and wondered what the boys would say if my father struck out.

The pitch came in. From the moment it left Brother Romo's hand, I knew it would be a good one to hit—belt high, slow, big as the moon, and my father with a bat the size of a Douglas fir in his hand.

And hit it my father did.

The ball rose on a line, over the second baseman's head, and seemed to gain altitude after that. The right fielder and center fielder both looked panicky, then turned their backs to us and began to run. I stared. Just stared. My father. My father had hit that ball. He had hit the ball a long, long way. Practically knocked the cover off it.

"Better run now, Neal, if you want us to win this game."

I was so stunned that I had forgotten to run. My father

had jogged down to first base and gently reminded me that I'd better get moving. My arms churned and my legs started to spin. I ran as hard as I could, around second, around third, my chest heaving, my wonder skyrocketing. It seemed the whole ward's eyes were upon me. No athlete in the World Series had ever experienced a moment such as that, sprinting toward home, the game-winning run in the ward Pioneer Day celebration. Mays and Mantle had nothing on me.

I slid into home plate, more for effect than necessity. Bishop Ranstrom laughed and called the game over. The outfielders were only then catching up with the ball. My father stood at first base and looked especially pleased with himself. He knew he only needed to get to first, and it was not his way to draw attention to himself or take more than he needed.

I slowly arose and dusted myself off, happy, complete, triumphant, a champion.

Bishop Ranstrom clapped me on the shoulder. "Nice base running, Neal. At least, once you decided to get started. Quite a hit your father had. Hope nobody is mad at the umpire, though I expect Brother Romo might be a few minutes late to bishopric meeting tomorrow. He'll get over it."

"Thanks, Bishop. My dad. Wow. He sure hit it. That went a mile. I didn't know . . ."

Bishop Ranstrom looked amused.

"I suppose your father's never mentioned it to you. He's too modest of a man. But it wasn't that long ago that Hal Rogers was maybe the finest high school baseball player in the city. First baseman and center field. College potential, they said, but the war kind of got in his way."

I looked toward my father, who had left his perch on first base and was folding our picnic blanket and calling my sisters. The game was over. The picnic was over. He had never told me he played baseball in high school.

He hit the ball a mile. At least.

The look of shock on the outfielders' faces as the ball screamed over their heads.

And my father had seen that I had arrived home safely. The game-winning run.

———

In my earliest recollections, I see my father coming home after work, worn and slumped, often with nicks and cuts on his forearms, his face and hands grimy because when you make boxes and run the machines that make boxes, in the air there is dirt and dust and exhaust from the machines, and you come home with it all over you, and to me, looking back all these years, the layer of grime worn by my father was like a hard-earned royal robe.

He never complained about work, the people there, the pay he received.

———

"Bishop Ranstrom says you were a good ballplayer, Dad."

"I played a little."

"But you were good."

"I enjoyed it."

"He said you were maybe the best in Portland. You never told me. You never told me about it."

He looks into the backseat of our car, where Tom and

Rosie are already asleep, worn out from the Pioneer Day picnic. Mother nods and smiles and reaches for his shoulder and pats him.

"You never said anything about it," I repeated. "Why?"

"You never asked."

I am a technical writer. It's what I do for a living. I sit in a cubicle and I try to make complicated things easier to understand. I do not make boxes. And the challenges I face, the disappointments, the vague dissatisfaction, the feeling of longing that sometimes leaves me blue, I wonder what my father would think of it, I wonder how he would handle it, I wonder what advice he would dispense to me, this man who made a million boxes and more, and, by doing so, kept us in clothes and food and whatever else was essential to us.

I cannot yet say what I make in this life. I wonder if the footprint of my life is shallow, or deep, or if it is there at all. He could say that he made millions of boxes, proof of his life's work, square and sturdy and needed and useable.

He once told me he wanted to go to college. He wanted to be an architect. In his dreams, he must have seen skyscrapers. The vision of that—my father on campus, books under his arm, hurrying among classes, wild, daring, brilliant dreams of his own, bold and flashing, chasing them down—crept upon me a few years back, caught up with me in an unguarded moment. I was sitting on an airplane, bound for St. Louis. And the tears came, and they rolled all the way down and landed softly on my suit, and no one around me could have imagined why the grown man in seat 14b was quietly crying.

I could do what my father only dreamed of, and he could not do it because he went to war twice and came home and had a wife and children to care for. He built us a home. That's what he did when he came home from war. He didn't go to school, he didn't become an architect, and he never made a fortune.

With him, the other things came first, and as his child, I was among those things that came first. What would this box-maker, someone who worked with his hands and worked on machines, to make sure all the corners were square and the seams tight, what would he tell me now?

If I could be part of the man he was. My father made boxes. I write technical manuals and instructions on how to install computer software. I would like to write a book some-day. I would like to be an architect. These are my dreams, and they make me feel foolish and they make me feel strong, as our unrealized dreams do for all of us. And maybe our success can be measured by what we learned from dreaming. Or our dreams can haunt us, tracing a gritty black outline to our lives, the colors inside not filled in. There may be no better way to understand a man or woman than to understand what they dream and why they dream what they do. There may be no better way to understand a man or a woman and why they stopped pursuing their dream or why they didn't start at all.

My father wanted me to be an architect, he wanted me to be something he could never have the chance to do. He never said that's what he wanted me to become, but a son feels what his father wants for him and no words ever need to be spoken. Once, I told him, I told him of this small dream of mine, to write a book, a book that everyone would read and everyone would like. He said nothing about architecture, he only nodded and said, "I think you can do it, Neal. I think you can. You'll be a fine writer, I reckon." I never told him the book I wanted to write was about him.

Time, you can't slow it down, and dreams, you can stop pursuing them, but you can never quite kill them. Men my age should know those things. I can still write that book, and the book might be like the boxes my father built, things that last, things that are important.

I have other dreams. Sometimes, I dream of lawns.

Lawns, you make them green, and the grass comes up long after you fertilize it, and if it all works as it should, boys come up and grow from the lawn, too. It seems that way. A funny dream it is, when I close my eyes and see boys growing straight and tall as if they were blades of grass, and how, if they are trod or trampled on, they are resilient and come back up. My father dreamed that dream, and so did Brother Hutton, and Brother Newell learned about it, too. And then they made that dream come true.

A man can dream of making boxes. I know that. My father made boxes. The Savior was a carpenter. I wonder if He ever created a wooden box. I think He must have. What tender care He must have used in creating his boxes, to make sure the corners fit and were tight and that they would last a long time. His boxes lasted for eternities.

We were never late for church. My father has something to show for his life.

The boxes he made.

CHAPTER 5

March 1956

Sometimes, I drift back to those earlier days, back to the neighborhood I grew up in. I envision the houses and the people who lived on my street. I think of the pretty lawns and the way the plum trees flowered in the spring. I remember the paint on each of the houses, always white, except when Mr. Barney got bold one summer and painted his home a light tan, which set the neighbors clucking.

"It's too different. Surprised Maureen went along with it."

"Makes his house stand out. Didn't think Dale was the kind to call attention to himself. Guess maybe he is."

"I like it. Might paint mine blue next summer."

"Oh, you can't. You wouldn't dare. Gina would never let you. Blue. My word."

And always the games played on the street.

"Let's play ball."

"Not enough guys today. Just four of us."

"Get Joey."

"Can't. He's gone to Pendleton to see his cousins."

"We can play five-hundred. Fly ball is one-hundred."

"Fifty for one hop."

"Twenty-five for two."

"Nothing for three. Batter has to swing up. Can't hit grounders."

"Okay. Batter has to swing up. No grounders. Three grounders in a row and you can't bat anymore."

"Can't hit away from anyone."

"No, can't do that."

"Let's go. Who bats?"

"We'll play bottle up to see."

I can remember the old church building, too, and what went on there. Sometimes, with eyes closed, I take myself back there.

Where am I? What room am I near?

A door is to my right. I lean toward it, and in neat rows, see small chairs. I imagine, imagine small, serious children, seated, arms folded, on a bright Sunday morning. Sweetly singing of popcorn and prophets, of sunbeams and flowers, innocent as angels, their sound seems to fill the room, wispy as clouds, tangible as the hard wood floor beneath their feet. Years go by, years in a blink and flash.

For a few minutes, I am back in my home ward. Back to one of my first memories of the old chapel covered in ivy.

Sister Glynn sits in a big chair, with a half dozen little chairs around her in a semicircle. She is a large woman, with strawberry-blonde hair, uncomfortable on the chair, uncomfortable with the lesson topic. Her hands, I remember her hands, and her thick, stout fingers. She nervously fidgets in her chair—we wiggle in ours and wonder what she will say and what we will do next. I am five years old, and Sister Glynn, freshly baptized, working in her first church calling, is trying to explain the Resurrection to her class of Sunbeams.

It is not an easy lesson to teach. When you are new in the Church. Or when you are old in the Church.

"You see, it's like this," she says, and then stops. How do you explain the miracle of resurrection to five-year-olds? How do you tell them about death and life, cruelty unmatched, love pure and unfeigned, especially when you are new to the Church yourself and perhaps not all that sure of the principles you are trying to teach?

She holds out her hands and spreads her fingers—little, stubby, pink-not-quite-red. She turns her palms upward. She says, "Okay." Then she doesn't speak for a few seconds.

"Let me explain it like this," she says and then she says no more, and she looks up, and we instinctively look up, too. She closes her eyes. Ours remain wide open.

———

My father liked the Glynns. He said they were good people. I remember he went to their baptism with my mother.

My father always liked the underdogs, and face it, new in the Church meant you were an underdog in some ways.

I look at my shoes, I look at my socks, and I play with the little clip-on bow tie that my mother attached to my shirt. I look through the window and see daffodils in full bloom, yellow and green, popping straight into the air. It was spring, it had to be spring in Oregon, when the daffodils burst forth and gulped in the fresh March air.

"This is hard," says Sister Glynn. "I have two children of my own, a little older than all of you, and I don't quite know how to say this and make sense and make it so that you'll understand."

A head pops into the room, and a Primary counselor, Sister Stephenson, asks, "All okay in here, Sister Glynn?"

"Yes, yes. Everything is fine. It's a nice class, and we're having a good time," she says. She looks as if she wants to say something else, but stops. Then she repeats slowly, "We're having a good time, an interesting discussion with these five-year-olds," and Sister Stephenson smiles and nods and softly closes the door.

"This is about Jesus, and how He died and what happened next to Him," she says.

I think of the painting of Him in the back of the chapel and how He holds a lamb close to him. Then I take off my bow tie and look out the window at the flowers, and the other children squirm and touch each other, and we don't quite understand why we are there and what we are supposed to learn.

We are underdogs, too.

We wait for Sister Glynn to say something, to tell us to do something, and we wonder about how Jesus died, though we all know that a cross was part of it.

Sister Glynn looks up again and closes her eyes and then says, "I have an idea."

We stop wiggling for a moment, and she smiles, a large smile that fills the room with warmth and, I think, causes the daffodils to stretch and reach even more toward heaven. She opens her hands and spreads her fingers wide and says, "Everything is so simple. I understand that now. All so simple."

She says, "Bad men didn't like Jesus, and they tricked some people into telling them where He was.

"He was in a garden, and He was praying. The bad men took Jesus to a hill and there was a cross made of wood."

She stops and looks into our faces, one by one. She has our attention. She is about to say something to us, this large, good lady, ruddy-complexioned, huge in heart, huge in spirit.

"The bad men . . ." and she pauses. Years later, I realize that she cannot say, "spikes" or "nails," she absolutely cannot, she must say something, yes, for us, but also for her own tender feelings.

"They put pins in Jesus' hands and feet and they hung Him on the cross and He died."

She looks again to the ceiling, and again, I realize, years later, revelation coming to me, sometimes in big things, sometimes in small, but all with meaning, that she is praying over each word that she will speak to us. Our shoulders hunch. This being, whom we hear of each week, the picture in the back of the chapel, the image of mildness, He died.

"But it is okay that He died because He lived again."

And so He did. He lived again. And it was all okay. I understood. We understood.

Sister Glynn leans back and she, too, is relieved, and the pure, coursing joy of the moment seems to envelop us all. He lived, He died, He lives again. She looks up at the ceiling one more time. It was that simple, and we understood.

That happened. It happened in the room where the Primary met. Miracles of understanding happen, they happen all around us, and they can happen to a teacher, a new teacher, and they can happen to five-year-olds, transfixed by our teacher in red, who thought it good to pray once, twice, three, and four times, before telling her class about the Resurrection.

Sister Glynn and her family moved away a few years later. She had another baby, that much I recall; and they moved to a small town on the coast. I remember someone saying that they were doing well and her children were happy, and they were all active and that her husband might have been in a bishopric.

And I think, *That's how her life should be. She was a gifted teacher and a good, good lady.*

"Lost ball."

"Where is it? Where did the ball go?"

"I don't know. It went over into Mrs. Munson's hedge. It's in her flower bed."

"Can't find it."

"I'll come and help. You, too, Rusty."

"What if we can't find it?"

"We'll be done."

"No more baseballs?"

"I don't have any more."

"Any money?"

"Not enough. We could trade in some pop bottles."

"We did that last week. No more pop bottles."

"Lost ball."

"Game's over."

"Lost ball."

"I have some boards in my garage. Let's build something. Let's get some nails, and you bring your dad's hammer and I'll get my dad's, and we'll build something. We could build a ship and float it on the mud puddle by DeAngelo's. Game's over. Lost ball."

"Okay. Meet you at your garage."

———

And I have sat in lessons in Gospel Doctrine class, and I have sat in lessons in priesthood meeting, and I have heard teachers talk about the Crucifixion, and they have made their point by bringing in huge nails and spikes and letting us hold them and feel their weight. And they have said, "This is about the size and weight of the nails used on the cross." And I have shuddered at the brutality of it all, the horrible irony of how the Prince of Peace died. The movies they make, the ones that show the long spikes pressed against the soft flesh of hands, waiting the heavy and final judgment of a stone hammer aiming true to its mark.

At such times, I close my eyes and think of a Primary class long ago and a teacher who prayed at the right time and got her answer.

And I prefer, for good or not, to think of pins, not spikes, and how it was okay, because He did, after all, live again.

———

When the cry would go up, "Lost ball!" we'd stop our game and spend many anxious minutes searching for the ball. We'd look in the bushes, under cars. We'd look in the trees, even in the milk boxes on our back porches. We'd look in crawl spaces under houses, and in basement window wells. We'd look in mud puddles. We detested a ball that found its way to Mrs. Munson's hedge, where dozens of balls met their demise in the thick, prickly greenery. We'd enlist any other boys on the block to help us, and girls, too. You find the lost ball, and we'll give you candy or we'll give you a nickel or we'll give you the chance to bat.

And then, when we were about to give up, when we were hopeless, sometimes, at the last possible second, someone would spot the ball, and the game would be resumed, with joy.

The game went on, its life renewed. He died, He rose. From something lost to something found, something destroyed to something restored.

From lost ball to found ball, and then the game, and our life, went on.

CHAPTER 6

November 1966

There are the tall heroes, the ones right there, always, as I grew up. My parents. The Bishop Ranstroms. The Brother Huttons. The fathers and mothers in my neighborhood. My own sisters and brother. And then there are those who dash into your life here and there, now and again, and they teach a lesson that burns something good into your heart, and then they are gone again.

My mind flits back to my old ward house again, and I begin to daydream, almost as if I were there. In my imagination, I squeeze an old metal door handle and pull back and begin to walk up stairs, creaky and twisty. I had forgotten about this stairway, the secret stairway that led to the back of the stage at the front of the recreation hall. I feel along the wall and find a light switch and flip it on. An old brass fixture sprays feeble yellow light up the stairs. The air is musty, and my mind dips into a torrent of memories, to roadshows and ward plays, dances and balls, wedding receptions, and ward dinners.

"A floor show. What is a floor show?"

I will soon enough find out. My mother's voice comes to me, clearly, firmly.

"You will be part of the floor show for the ward Gold-and-Green Ball. You're going to dance. You'll be part of a dance group made up of other kids from Mutual."

She is in the car and we are driving home after Sunday School.

There is no escape for me.

She says, "Sister Austin asked me about you today. She said she needs a couple of more boys for the floor show. I told her you would be happy to help her out." She didn't say it, she didn't need to, but her words were almost palpable in the air: *That's it. No debate. Finished. I have made up my mind. Your direction is clear and it is set.*

Father, my usual ally, keeps his eyes on the road, his hands on the wheel, and his lips close together. There are times to make a stand, but he, calculating and weighing all things in this little circumstance, decides this is not one of them. His boy will rise in triumph or fall in ignominious defeat on his own at the ward Gold-and-Green Ball. His boy will take a girl by the hand and gracefully whirl and glide across the old parquet floor, or he will stumble and trip and fall before the entire ward. It is a thought not lacking some humor. From my position in the back of our family station wagon, I see his stoicism slip, and the faintest of smiles spreads across his face as Mom says, "You can hardly say no to Pamela Austin. And she took dance classes down at the Y, so she knows what she is doing. And what you'll learn will help you later on. It will give you the skills you will need to develop. You will thank us later in life."

Father, eyes again staring at the road straight ahead, says, "Pamela Austin is a formidable woman." And he need not have said it aloud, and the unspoken words hang stiff and clear in the air, *And so is your mother.*

So it came to be that ten days later, I had my sweating hands locked and pressing in those of Cathy Jo Carlson's as we listened to Sister Austin issue her commands. "You take a girl like this," she demonstrates to an odd lot of assorted teens, using one poor deacon as a model. "You put one hand square on her back, the other, that would be your left hand, boys, you use to hold her right hand. Your left, boys, her right. Got that? Neal, no death grips. You're going to cut off the circulation in Cathy Jo's hand and arm."

Sister Austin, square-jawed, short hair, hands on hips, not large, but certainly not small, *stout* perhaps being the best word to describe her. The mother of five, four of them girls, each reared to be a lady, and her one son, his course charted to be an old-school gentleman from the instant the doctor in the delivery room spanked him once and said, "It's a boy, Mrs. Austin. Congratulations."

We were, truth be told, a little intimidated by her. Perhaps a lot intimidated by her. She expected the best from those around her. She did not suffer fools, and fools aplenty there seemed to be close by, especially that night and in the persons of those of us who held the priesthood of Aaron, not to mention a girl in our arms for the first time.

"Stand up, straight, ready position, move with grace. We need more grace in this world. You deacons, go home and look up the word in the dictionary. Grace, I said. Grace it is. Now, on the beat, ready. Grace."

She stared at us, sharp-eyed, waspish, commanding. We moved tentatively. We looked at each others' feet. Grace was not in our vocabulary.

But another story of Sister Austin here, an explanation of why our Church needs those who are part silk, part steel.

I was a young boy, five or six years old. Measles had struck our family—my sisters, brother, myself, and, most surprisingly, my father. It was especially fearsome for my father, and I could sense, through Mother's expression, the gray lines on her face, the calls and consultations from doctors, that Father was very ill and that she was far more worried than she chose to say. We were a family downed by the illness, debilitated. Mother could not keep up with our needs.

And measles being measles in that era, people stayed away, fearful of the consequences of contact with our family. So we suffered through the illness that gripped our family, and in those days, in that place, you did not ask for help. You endured. If people had crossed the winter plains with rags on their backs and sagebrush husks on their feet, and had dug up roots through frozen ground to eat, you did not ask for help because your family had broken out with small red dots and fevers. You just didn't. Many of our neighbors were fighting the same battle and could offer little or nothing. It was a time when each family was on its own.

No matter that measles could kill, especially someone my father's age.

Then, a knock at the door one chilly night, and there, in the pale white light on our porch, stood Sister Austin, two bags of groceries on one arm, a pot of soup slung over the other.

Mother said, "Marjorie, you shouldn't be here. You'll get the measles or someone in your family will."

Sister Austin's no-nonsense reply was, "Fiddle. You need help, and I am here to give it, so I'll hear no more of your protests. I'll show my way to your kitchen." And in she swept, grand in her manner, with her groceries and soup and endless good will, impervious to the weak objections of my mother. And perhaps it was just the timing and that we had already rounded a corner in a battle with the measles, or maybe it was just the effect of care and concern, but whatever the truth of the matter, we began, with spirits on the rise, to heal. That very night. The small red dots began to go away, but the memory of Sister Austin and her groceries and her soup and her compelling manner has remained with me more than three decades later.

Sister Austin never got the measles. No measle would dare to show up on her.

"Gentlemen. You have a ways to go. Young ladies, I have confidence in you. It is always easier to teach girls. They are so much smarter than boys. But you know what? In the end, when I have the chance to teach dance, it is the boys who end up the best dancers. Stick with it, gentlemen, and remember . . . grace."

––––––––––

And a second story of the indomitable Sister Austin.

A year or so after the ward Gold-and-Green Ball. A group of men were huddled in one corner of the recreation hall just before the start of Sunday School. In another corner was a brother whose name I don't recall, perhaps because he was seldom seen at church. About him hung the unmistakable stench of acrid tobacco, partially camouflaged by aftershave. Sallow, unsure, he stood by himself. He looked at the group of men across the room from him, huddling for safety.

Sister Austin marches in and sizes up the situation. She strides across the hall and greets the brother, takes him by the hand, and tells him where Sunday School class is. He thanks her, then turns and shuffles down the hallway to where the class will meet.

Sister Austin walks by the knot of cowering men, eyes straight ahead, her pace brisk and unbroken. She says, just above a whisper, but with arrow-straight gravity, "Can't smell dishonesty. Can't smell immorality. Can't smell unclean thoughts. Can't smell cowardliness."

The men look up, look down, their faces ashen, as the arrow finds its target, square in the middle of their consciences.

Grace, a noun, unmerited assistance, pleasing in appearance or effect; the quality or state of being considerate, thoughtful, polite.

Grace, a verb, Sister Austin at our doorstep during a cold winter night, with food to eat and spirits to elevate.

It would have been too easy, too bereft of challenges, and our earthly experiences minimized, for the Lord to give the priesthood to the sisters and leave the brethren to their own devices.

"Beginning position. Left foot ready. Neal, hold Cathy Jo's hand higher. She will not bite you. She will not tromp on your feet. There is no need to fear. You will not touch any place on her that you shouldn't. You will not need to repent of this, though you will of other things. You are about to dance, not about to begin a march across Wyoming in winter," she says, pushing her thin-rimmed glasses higher on her nose, her eyes hawk-sharp, missing nothing. "Look as though you are enjoying yourself. You will in time. Remember, when people dance, the spectators look first at their faces, not at their feet. Your smile will set the stage, not your feet."

Cathy Jo is three years older and four inches taller than I am. Tall, willowy, graceful. It became clear to me, some years later, that Sister Austin had paired the strong with the weak. Cathy Jo did not, I assume to this day, want to be there any more than I, especially given the obvious inadequacies of her dance partner. But her grace was not limited to merely the way she moved. Grace, it seems, is contagious.

"You're a really good dancer, Neal."

"Not yet, he isn't. But he's improving, and I see occasional flashes of potential."

Sister Austin didn't miss anything.

"Music. Let's begin. We will stay until I see improvement. The harder you work, the sooner we will be done. The choice is yours, my young friends. Neal, you're going to cut off the circulation in Cathy Jo's hand. I have spoken to you about that before. We do not want that. It would not be a good thing."

And so it went. We practiced a dozen times. Gradually, the mystery of music, movement, and rhythm came to me, as it did to the others. Cathy Jo, good sport that she was, always made me feel comfortable. "You dance so smoothly," she told me. "You should keep dancing after this is over. I can't believe how much you've learned since last time."

She made me feel handsome.

The night of the ward Gold-and-Green Ball arrives. From the hallway, we peek into the recreation hall, and the sight overwhelms us. The room is decorated as we've never seen it before—long streamers of crepe paper, a mirrored, revolving ball, and a real band on the stage. Red punch flows from a silver fountain, and a gaudy table is weighed down with food. But the people were the more impressive sight. The people you saw at church on Sunday, ordinary, the man who sang too loud in sacrament meeting, the lady who always looked so tired. The dewlapped, gray-haired high priests, who all wore dark suits and skinny black ties. Their matronly wives, serious, furrowed, foreboding. They, and more, all of the faces you saw each Sunday.

But now, but now they are transformed: The white dinner jackets, the black tuxedo here and there, the long, flowing gowns of regal blue and silver, corsages, boutonnieres, slick black shoes, tall high heels matched in color to the ladies' wraps and purses. I see these people as they must have looked when they were younger. I see them laugh and smile and sway to the music and look at each other in ways that I never witnessed on Sundays.

We have more than a Sunday life.

This is it, this is what these Gold-and-Green Balls are about. For the men to look handsome and gallant, and the women to look beautiful and refined. For all of them to see each other in a different and a prettier light, to step out, to step away, to step up. The air in the recreation hall seems light, fizzy, a touch of the euphoric. The music is slow and earnest and slightly off-key. And from this combination of things that don't mix—heady high spirits in a usually sober group, older people looking young, and plodding music— comes a sparkly magic.

Cathy Jo taps me on the shoulder. "We'll be fine," she says. "You dance well."

Sister Austin, in her deep purple gown, gathers us together, chicks to a hen. "We go on in five minutes. You'll be wonderful. Your parents and others will see you in a way they have not seen you before. This will be a floor show they will all remember."

It is a transformation for us, too. A skinny, slightly short, scruffy teacher will be part of the floor show, and he will dance with grace.

I lower my head and look at myself. Blue suit, belonging to my father, hemmed up. A little baggy on me, a little tall for me. Dark shoes. White shirt. A bright red tie and bright red handkerchief tucked in my suitcoat pocket. Around me, the other boys are dressed similarly. Cathy Jo wears a pink fluffy gown, white shoes, her hair up and big. She wears perfume, rose, I think, although all perfumes smell like roses to me. She also looks different, prettier, and I hope that is partly because of me.

We will dance. We will dance together.

From outside the hall, we hear Brother James, and he's saying things to make the people laugh. Then he says more seriously, "And tonight . . ."

I adjust my tie. Cathy Jo smiles at me, then gives me a wink.

" . . . and you'll recognize some of these dancers, but they'll look different to you . . ."

I stand tall, as tall as I am able. I glance around the hallway we are in. The other boys seem as nervous as I am, which brings a welcomed feeling of relief. I look at Cathy Jo and think she is the prettiest girl I have ever seen, and I wish I were three years older and five inches taller.

" . . . they've worked hard preparing for the floor show tonight, so let's warmly welcome . . ."

Sister Austin whispers, "It's time to go, chins high, smiles on your faces, remember the ready position . . ."

" . . . our very own . . ." and the rest of his words are washed away in the warmth of applause.

Sister Austin says, "Now. Make your entrance, ladies and gentlemen. Make it grand."

So we do, marching purposely to our assigned positions, smiles plastered on our faces, feeling the excitement in the air as we become a part of the festivities, a part of the evening to remember.

A record player, a loudspeaker. These are the times before

sophisticated stereo equipment. We hear the needle drop on the record. Scratchy noises for a second or two, then the first note of our dance, part foxtrot, part samba, part waltz, part pure Sister Austin.

Cathy Jo seems to glide. From the corner of my eye, I see the other six couples. All is well. We move as one. No one hesitates. No one looks at his feet or for clues from nearby couples. We are confident. A miracle, right here in our old recreation hall. A lovely, hushed silence descends upon the room, other than the slightly static sound of the record, the gentle swish of pink dance skirts, the light tapping of our feet upon the parquet floor.

And parents in the room think, *Who are these young people? Who are they? They are our own. We have never seen them like this. Never. They are our own.*

I can dance, I can dance, I inwardly exult. Revelation comes at times in fantastic ways. The flushed feeling of success envelops me. They are watching us. We are a part of the night.

The music, I understand the music, what comes next, where I must be, what I must do. I seem to float. Cathy Jo is a cloud, a cirrus cloud, high above, wispy and delicate. She is beautiful, and I am handsome, and we are dancing. I do not need to look at the crowd. The hushed silence tells me that Sister Austin is correct. They are seeing us as they have never seen us before.

I feel grace.

And all of it comes to an end too soon. Our perfect dance is over. The clapping begins politely, then becomes thunderous, as we bow and begin our precise march off the dance floor. Our parents and the others stand and applaud as we stride away.

I wish we had a way, a way today, to see each other in such light again. We have more than our lives on Sunday. We need ways to show it.

What happened to Cathy Jo? What experiences has she had? What stories does she tell? And silly as it seems, I want her to be in a warm place, adored by a family, honored for the kind person she is. I want her to be free of despair and disappointment. I want only fair, soft winds in her life. I hope she occasionally thinks back to the floor show, perhaps when she walks into a cultural hall or a youth activity, and remembers the awkward boy she danced with. I hope she thinks, *I was kind to him,* and knows, somehow, that I also understand that. Kindness is never quite complete until it is recognized because only then can it be passed on.

Somewhere in the audience is my mother, happy and proud in her light blue gown; and my father, handsome in his best dark suit. She wears a flower. He wears a boutonnière. This boxmaker and his bride. After the dance, they will both spend some time in the kitchen, cleaning up, because that is the way they are. Then they will dance again, he tentative and self-conscious; she, feeling like a girl once more, glowing. After the ball, they will stop for dessert at a small restaurant near Powell Street, not far from our home. Later, they will hold each other and quietly talk into the deep black hours— about the dance and who was there and how everyone looked.

And they will touch and caress each other and be playful and then fall into sweet dreams.

Sister Austin says, "You were wonderful. Simply wonderful. I am so proud and happy for each of you."

At home, in the morning, on our dining room table, I see a rumpled corsage and small white carnation side-by-side, their fragrance only slightly diminished by the overnight hours.

Many years later, and I can still hear the tapping of shoes, the sound of the record. I still remember the song. The room in that old building now is probably still and dark. How it sparkled one night, so many years ago. You would not know it now, you would not guess it.

And with that memory comes another: one star followed in spectacular orbit by a second of no less than equal brilliance.

From across another room, in a different place, nine years later. I walk slowly toward a pretty girl, and when I reach her, I ask her to dance. The music this night is also slow. I take her right hand in my left. I place my hand lightly on her back. I assume the ready position, as Sister Austin taught me so long ago.

"I should tell you. My name is Neal."

She says, "My name is Amanda. Amanda, plain-old-Smith."

"It's a pretty name, Amanda, plain-old-Smith."

A few minutes later, when the music slows, fades, and

ends, she says, "You dance very well, Neal. Much better than anyone else here."

I have danced with grace.

She is at home now, this Amanda, who dances well. She has experienced some good times in her life and loved them; she has endured some difficult times and learned from them. I danced with her that night so many years ago. She teaches English at a junior high, and she loves to read. Her love of words and slow turning of pages as evening creeps toward us has proved contagious. New worlds we have discovered together, through the volumes we have read.

She knows I want to write a book. She says she thinks I can do so. Where we live now, the temperature is eight degrees. It is clear outside, but a week-old snow lingers. There is a family with illness, all four of the children and the mother, too. They live a mile away from us. One of the sick children is a pupil of Amanda's.

The soup is ready. The bread, fresh-baked and fragrant, is wrapped in a clean dishtowel and in a paper bag. She has a pitcher of orange juice, too.

Amanda nods. "This flu is contagious and can be dangerous," she says. "You didn't get your shot," she says.

So, I say. "I hate shots. So . . ."

"Yeah. So. Let's go."

"Okay. Ready."

Into the brittle night we plunge, and we can hear the sounds of twigs cracking on the trees and snow crunching beneath our feet, and, in the distance, from somewhere in the rimrock, a coyote yelp. The moon is a bright pale yellow, like a cold marble suspended in the sky.

Minutes later, we hold each other close, almost if we were dancing, our arms interlocked tightly, as we walk up the slippery driveway toward the stricken family's house—soup, bread, juice, and optimism held in precarious balance. Our way is lighted only by a feeble lamp from inside the home.

The driveway is long. The wind tears and bites, and the snow, whipped up from the ground, feels like gravel blown against our faces. We trudge ahead.

We go forward with grace.

CHAPTER 7

January 1966

When I was growing up, it was unusual for anyone in our neighborhood to sell their home. Back in those days, you bought a house and you stayed in a house and that was that. Your home was as much a part of you as any of your physical characteristics—the way you looked, the way you walked, the way you spoke, the wrinkles on your forehead, the color of your eyes. Your house was like a name. That's why we were all surprised when the "For Sale" sign went up on the Neelands' home during the dead of one winter.

Besides, Corky Neeland was a friend of mine. I did not want him to move.

"Why are you moving?"

"Don't know."

"Do you know where?"

"Out toward Gresham. My dad wants to build a house. So does my mom. Guess we'll move."

"I guess. I hope they play baseball on the street out there."

Corky looked doubtful. "There's a park. It's part of the neighborhood. I don't think we'll play on the street. I think we'll play in a park."

"That's different. I guess it won't hurt as much when you fall down."

"Nope, guess not."

The buildings you lived in, the buildings you went to school in, the buildings you went to church in. They were like blocks of granite in your life—things that don't change. Looking back, my three sisters and my brother and I all went to the same elementary school, the same high school, and the same church building until we were old enough to go away to college. And my parents lived in the same white house their entire adult lives. I remember my mother opening a letter from the bank one Saturday morning and saying, "Oh, my. I didn't realize it. We own our house now. It's paid for."

The house must have seemed large to them when my youngest sister finally graduated from high school and began college. By then, one bathroom was plenty. My father could finally set up a shop in the basement. He kept the lawn green. You never knew when boys, your own or someone else's, might want to play hide-and-seek. Or maybe your grandchildren. Times changed, children grew up, moved away. But your home and your church were always there, and the children always returned, even if only for brief visits.

I remember more about that old church building and what went on inside it.

I remember sitting on the grand stairway that led from the large, wood double-doors to the chapel entrance. I remember waiting for adults who visited with one another after meetings. It was a natural place to congregate, on those stairs, between the chapel and the front doors. I remember sitting with friends and talking. I remember Bishop Ranstrom occasionally stopping by and sitting down with us on the stairway and joining our conversations. I remember my father on those stairs, helping one of the older, gray-haired sisters to the chapel. I remember how, when a few of us, no doubt bored with a speaker at sacrament meeting, would find an excuse to leave the chapel, and, with no adult watching, would sit with our legs extended, and in our slick, polyester church pants, slide down the sleek, wood stairs before dutifully returning to the meeting, smug in the thought that no one had seen us. The stairs were a crossroads, situated between the front doors and the chapel and the recreation hall. It was the perfect place for a boy to keep track of the comings and goings in the ward. Occasionally, we were the first to see people new to our ward walk into that fine old building.

A cold, windy day in January. A couple of inches of snow on the ground, rare for the mild Oregon climate. I am fourteen years old, a teacher in the Aaronic priesthood, perched on the stairway with two friends, a little before Sunday School was to begin. One of the big wood doors swings open, letting in, first, a blast of the icy east wind and then a rail-thin young man, a little older than I. His dark eyes dart from one side of the room to the other, then up the stairs. He blinks. His eyes seem to rest upon me. He takes two steps my way and says in a mild voice with an unmistakable Japanese accent, "My name is Seiji Inahara. I am from Hokkaido. In America, they call me Sam. This is the LDS Church?"

I nod and say, "Yes, this is the LDS Church." And for some reason, with maturity or insight beyond my age, or maybe just a wild, lucky impulse, I add, "Welcome."

It was different in those days. Shadows from World War II, dark and ragged, still hung over the land. No family, it seemed, was untouched by the war years and the deep wounds they had inflicted. Healing had begun, from the outside working in, but the healing was far from complete. It had not yet reached all the way into all of the people of that generation.

My father was not without such scars. Gentle by nature, playful, naïve, rising above the hardship of the Great Depression and riding a wave of optimism, he had moved to the city from the farm he had grown up on in eastern Oregon. And it started so well. His first job, driving a truck for a paper goods company. His first apartment, snug against the West Hills, sixth floor, a view of the city. His first car, a 1938 Chevy. A new set of clothes, tan linen sport coat, white buck shoes, a necktie with a palm-leaf pattern. And his first love, an auburn-haired girl from Idaho named Joy, the woman he would marry in a few years' time.

And then, only weeks after a fateful Sunday morning in December 1941—when ships were turned into blackened skeletons and some boys were never found, and others burned in the oil on the water, and others just never made it to the top deck and were forever entombed in the rusting husk of a vessel—he enlisted in the U.S. Navy, soon to be trained as a sailor and whisked to the South Pacific.

This is what he encountered, this is what he endured, two years after Pearl Harbor: his ship, sunk by a torpedo from a Japanese submarine, and eight terrifying hours, floating in dark, shark-infested waters until he was miraculously rescued.

One brother lost in the Philippines, assumed dead, on the long miserable march named for Bataan. Another captured, loaded onto a ship with other prisoners of war, all of whom perished when that ship sank after an American submarine's torpedo swirled and writhed and found its target, filled with human cargo, at midship. Sunk by "friendly fire," as it became known.

And my father came back from the war, and he tried to explain to his parents what he had seen, and he tried to see something larger, a bigger plan, to make sense of war. But he could not. It just happened. That's the way it all turned out. There was nothing more to say. It just happened and he was helpless to change it or make it different except in a small way, by serving his country and trying to stay alive. Ultimately, that's what he decided, you helped your country the most by staying alive.

He slept thereafter with his eyes open, and when he dreamed, his dreams were dark and flashed yellow-red, and the noise was thunderous, and from that time forward, he lived two lives: the one he had hoped for and the one the war wouldn't let him forget.

He married Joy, and went back to work, and tried to forget

some things and replace them with others. You have a bad memory, you live a nightmare, and you try to substitute dreams for them and hope one crowds out the other as time passes. Sometimes the plan worked and sometimes it did not. They had children and built a small white home in a modest part of the city.

He came home to a new job. He made boxes, and as he filled orders and fed the machine that creased and slit the fiber board in just the right places and gave the flat sheets form and purpose, he thought. He liked making boxes because the angles were clean and the lines on the flat boxes unerring, and in a world that was not tidy, he liked that a simple sturdy box could be fashioned, over and over again, until he had made millions of them. And while he made his boxes, he thought about his brothers, and he thought about his parents, and he thought about war. He thought about what he had seen and how he never wanted to see it again and how he never wanted anyone in any place to ever see it again.

He was a good boxmaker, and he rose through the ranks of the company and became in time its general manager. He never lost his fascination with simple boxes and how good and ordered the world of a box factory was, in contrast to the confusion and chaos he had experienced during those grim war years.

Later, when he was ill, and I sat by his bed, I once asked him, "Take me there. Tell me about the war. Tell me all the things you never would. Tell me what it was like because I want to know." And he said, "No. You do not need to know. I will not take you there." And he didn't.

But as a young man, at the machine that made the boxes, he thought about the people and the nation that had changed his life and the lives of each family member forever. When he was ill, toward the end, he looked up from his bed and called the names of his two brothers and said, "I am coming to you," and minutes later, he did just that. Father always kept his word.

We were never late for church.

My father was a boxmaker.

All of this, and Sam Inahara was about to become one of my lifelong friends.

"Sam, come home with us for Sunday dinner. My mother doesn't mind. She enjoys company. We put an extra plate on the table and that's that. All you have is to go back to the dormitory."

Sam smiles gently. "I cannot."

"You can."

"I cannot. I should not."

Sam cocks his head slightly and looks out on the lawn, the long, green lawn cared for by Roy Newell. It is spring now. Trees bloom with pink-and-white blossoms. Puffy clouds, some like boats, some like birds, all in a deep blue ocean, drift lazily in the sky.

"You can."

"I must be invited. It is not this way in my country. In Japan. It is different. You must be invited to a home. You do not come by and stay."

"You are invited. This is your invitation."

He squints. "No. It must be, the word is . . . formal."

"This is America. This is as formal as it gets. We could write you an invitation and mail it, but why bother? Just come to dinner. My parents won't mind."

My father says little about the war, his experiences. It wasn't until after his death that I found an old scrapbook in the garage attic, a yellow newspaper clipping, with a photo of a handsome young sailor and the headline: "War Hero Returns Home."

He says little about war because those who seem to say the most are those who have never been in one. He said little about war when our soldiers and sailors went off to fight in other wars, other than, when the newsreel at the movies showed scenes of war, he would shake his head ever so slightly and lower his jaw, and I would watch the moisture well in his eyes.

You can live through a war, but a war never leaves you, and you leave part of yourself on the battlefield or the ocean or somewhere in the air.

"It's just dinner, Sam. We eat it every Sunday after Sunday School. My family invites people over on Sundays all the time. You can stay with us in the afternoon, until sacrament meeting, then you can go with us to church."

Sam listens intently. We are on the rock steps out front of the church. I have tried to get Sam to our home for dinner for many weeks. A station wagon, wood-paneled, a Plymouth, rumbles by. Sam looks skyward and his shoulders sag a little, finally worn down by my insistence. "All right. I will go to your home for dinner." His concession seems to take a weight off him. He nods, not up, not down, more sideways. He smiles. "Will you eat, let me say, meat and potatoes?"

And so there are different cultures at work here, and an ocean between my country and his, and a war, freshly fought, between his country and my father.

Father knows that I am becoming friends with Sam. He knows that Sam occasionally helps me with math and often helps me with Spanish because Sam speaks his native tongue and Spanish and English and French, and when he leaves on a mission for Brazil three years hence, he will add Portuguese to his fluencies. He is here to study languages and words. He will one day translate pamphlets about the Church into many languages, and he will later on return to Japan and teach linguistics at a prominent university. He will further trace the origins of the Japanese language back to the Middle East and will become renowned for his linguistic genius.

But now, this complicated and convoluted mixing of culture and history is reduced to simplicities, a man, a young man, a boy, and a pot roast dinner with boiled red potatoes and green string beans.

And I am only vaguely aware of what is going on about me and how powerful memory is at work when Sam and I get out of his small car and walk up the driveway and toward the front door of my home.

To me, I am bringing home a new friend, a different friend, for Sunday dinner. That's all. He is kind and he is gentle, and he patiently helps me with my homework, and since I was born a few years after World War II, I do not understand the significance of his visit to our dinner table.

I have no enemies, of my own making nor inherited.

I knew, even then, that peace will never be achieved as long as people try to kill each other's children.

I do not understand the largeness of hearts, nor do I understand their smallness, but I am about to see something that, years later, will bring a nearly invisible tear to my eyes and a twisting ache welling up in my throat.

My father has watched me befriend Sam. He has watched from a distance. He has said nothing about Sam, other than two questions: What part of Japan is he from? He helps you with your school work, correct?

Now he stands at the doorway to our home, hands on hips, a thousand thoughts rushing in a thousand different directions. In the kitchen window, Mother looks pensive. Sam nods and talks and I cannot hear what he says, because it is as though a dark cloud has torn through the blue sky and sharks are swimming in that ocean of air and I sense that something may not be right. We walk toward the door, to the step. I look closely at my father, and his lips are drawn in a thin line and his pale blue eyes frosted with emotion.

He reaches his right hand out toward Sam.

He says, "Welcome, Seiji. Welcome to my home."

Sam looks surprised and pleased. "You call me Seiji. You call me by my Japanese name."

"Yes. It is Seiji. Is that right? Welcome. We are honored to have you here. I had hoped you would come and join us some-time."

"Yes. Seiji. I do not hear my Japanese name much in your country. My name is Seiji."

"Come in and tell us about yourself, Seiji. Come in and tell us about your family and your schooling and what led you to Oregon. How you became a Church member. Tell us about these things. We would like to get to know you better than we do." He pauses. The foreboding that I felt only seconds ago dissipates. Whatever was wrong, whatever could have been wrong, is no longer.

A war leaves the present and becomes history. It slips away. It vanishes.

Father says, "I am glad that you and Neal have become friends."

I have learned that greatness is not often born at the head of armies or standing before large gatherings of people. I have learned that it is only rarely manifested in grandiose words or bold action and that it has little to do with position or title or authority. Rather, true greatness most often comes from small turnings within the soul, in quiet ways, in actions that the world will little note. Greatness is around us, below us. It is not often above us. We need to reach down for greatness, where the small things are at our feet. It comes in small, simple words and sublime magnanimity: "Welcome, Seiji. Welcome to my home."

The meek will inherit the earth. The meek. No one else. Just the meek.

Only a handful of people knew of Gethsemane. None of them understood it.

———

Corky Neeland moved away in June, after his home sold. I never saw him again.

The Reeds moved into the Neeland home. Their son, Sid, became my friend.

What does this memory of Seiji and my father mean to me now? So much time has passed.

I have not lost a brother or a son in a vile war, as all wars ultimately are. I have not worn a uniform, I have not left my wife, expecting a child, and gone to a faraway land to fight. I have not been told who is my enemy and whom I must battle in a struggle that is difficult to understand. I have not taken the life of a man or a woman's son or daughter. My particular lot, compared with others, has not been as difficult to bear as that borne by the gallant generation one before mine.

I can only think this: *He was the Prince of Peace. He remains the Prince of Peace, and all things peaceful, all reconciliation is His.*

Even in my home, between a boy and a man from different sides of the vast ocean, His peace will reign, if we but allow it.

———

That was the first time Seiji Inahara visited our home, but it was not the last. Far from it. When he left on his mission a few years later, when he had his old-time missionary farewell at sacrament meeting, since his parents remained an ocean away and were not members of our faith, my father spoke at

Seiji's request, and he spoke of him as though he were his own son.

Father rises slowly from one of the red chairs to the left of the bishop. He has a sheet of paper in his hand. When he reaches the podium, he puts aside the paper. He brushes it away. What we plan to say is seldom the best thing we can say. He glances at Seiji and clears his voice and speaks in his smooth baritone.

Father spoke for five minutes. He spoke of brotherhood and forgiveness and love, kindness, and sacrifice. He wished Seiji success and gave him his blessing, and this boxmaker, I thought then and still think now, was perhaps the wisest man I have known, with his clean angles and clear creases, and the squareness of the life he made.

That we should all make boxes.

That I could be a part of what he was.

CHAPTER 8

September 1964

B ishop Ranstrom is a mailman. That is what we called them back in those days, not postal workers or letter carriers. They were known simply as mailmen. They brought us letters. They brought us messages. I remember his hands. They were large and thick, but also seemed gentle. His expression was that of a wry, patient man. He was given to smiling. His laughter was deep and contagious. All those years as bishop, and I saw him wear only two suits: a black one and another black one. If you looked closely, you could see a tiny herringbone pattern in one. His other suit was plain. He had a black tie and a blue tie, and toward the end of his service as bishop, his wife bought him a maroon-and-gray tie. Bishop Ranstrom must have often wondered if it were too fancy.

We cling to a little hope. President Kennedy is gone, but we have survived, and there is faint optimism among us. We withstood the worst and lived. The Dodgers win the World Series behind the magnificent left-armed wizardry of Sandy Koufax. The Beatles sing "I Want to Hold Your Hand" on *Ed Sullivan*. Father looks worried one night at dinner when he says, "China exploded an A-bomb today. Let's look at the news. We're not ready for this." Martin Luther King wins a Nobel Prize, and the Civil Rights Act is passed. A blonde-haired woman wiggles her nose and says she is a witch, and we all have a new favorite TV show. The surgeon general links smoking and cancer. Congress says it's okay to escalate the war in a place called Vietnam.

In our neighborhood, Robin Mitchell gets married to a boy named Tim Hutchins. Robin once was my babysitter. We played kick-the-can together, when I was little and she was older. She told me when to run, when I could dash to the can and kick it and be safe. "Now, Neal, run now, run hard!" she whispered. "You'll make it if you run now."

We still play baseball in the street, but some of the older boys seem to have lost interest. Paul Wilson faints in health class, when we're shown a filmstrip about babies being delivered. Johnny DeAngelo is seen holding Rhonda Russell's hand in the park after school.

I see Tim pull Robin close to him, his arm around her waist, in the Mitchells' backyard after their wedding reception, and I feel as though something is changing forever. Three months later, Tim joins the marines, to avoid being drafted into the army.

Those were days of change, and it caught me by surprise. No one had told me that each day would be a little different from the one that just passed and that tomorrow would be a little different from today. I had assumed that I had all the time in the world and that some things would always remain the same.

Until the day when the faint gnawing grows too loud to ignore and you mourn for times that you will never see again, and only hope that better things lie just ahead.

———

Bishop Ranstrom is a tall man, broad shouldered, with wavy brown hair, tinged with silver, combed straight back. He served as bishop for a long time—almost nine years. He speaks slowly, carefully choosing his words. I see him looking at the congregation, his eyes moving slowly during a sacrament meeting, coming to rest now and then on an individual, a faint change of expression—a slight nod, a small smile, a wrinkled forehead—as he thinks of the person and what he knows and what needs to happen next.

I am convinced that a good bishop, although it is yet to be written in any handbook or guideline, always knows what needs to happen next. For everyone. Everyone in his ward.

I think of him now, and the word that comes to me is *kindness*. He was, in my memory, unfailingly kind. And when all is said and thought of a bishop, he will be remembered and revered most for his kindness—that and knowing what needs to happen next.

Where he is now, I do not know; my mind does quick calculations: He would be, if alive, in his early eighties. Not impossible, but still not likely. Likely less that his roots are still in the Oregon soil, his home still in the lines on a map that demarcate my old ward. He is gone, as certainly as my family is also gone.

After my mission, after college, I began my own hopscotch path across the West and left my home for good. You keep in touch for a few months, you keep in touch maybe for a few years. But with rare exception, you lose contact, even with those who were good and kind, those who shaped you, those who could see, perhaps more clearly than you, what should come next in your life. I have not heard anything of Bishop Ranstrom for more than two decades. I hope he had a good life. If still alive, I hope he is well.

Let me try to drift backward in time, to run against the grain of nothing less than the power of the galaxies and the universe. I try to summon up a Sunday from many years ago.

It comes. Why this particular meeting, what triggered this memory, I don't know. But the thought comes, clear and happy.

My father says, "I like Jim Hopson. He is a good fellow."

Mother is less sure. "There is something about him. I don't know what it is. He's different, maybe that's the way to say it. He is not the kind of young man, I would say, who has much of a chance of getting married. He has no social skills. Can you imagine him on a date? They'd read a physics text-book. He wouldn't get the door for a girl and he wouldn't hold her hand. Or he would hold her hand when she didn't want him to. That's Jim. He has it all backwards."

Father had a different opinion. "Jim is different in your eyes because he is almost thirty years old and unmarried. His time will come. Then he'll seem as normal and well-adjusted as anyone else we know."

"All that education," Mother says.

Indeed, Jim is well-educated. He has four college degrees, he instructs physics at the nearby university, and long sentences with big words and big ideas that few of us have ever discovered flow from him as freely as water out of a gully after a long rain. Jim taught us in deacons quorum for a time, not long, and we ended up talking about the universe and relativity and movement of the planets and quarks and the realness and physical existence of time almost as much as we discussed anything vaguely resembling a gospel topic.

They were always interesting times when he taught, chalk in hand, drawing on the board, scribbling in big, loopy letters, ideas and words and chalkboard drawings, spinning out like trails of cosmic dust from the edge of a freewheeling galaxy. Jim wasn't showing off; that's just who he was, the way he thought, what he talked about. In deacons quorum, Jim brought us into his world, a strange, often bizarre and always exciting place.

And he often concludes one of his rambling, wild-ride, hold-on-to-your-seatbelt lessons by pushing his glasses higher on his nose and uttering in a tone both serious and exultant, "You see? You see how it all fits! You see how science and religion all work together? It's true!"

He is tall and thin. His reddish-blond hair and a comb remain relative strangers. He speaks rapidly, words bursting forth in a feverish flurry. His dark, skinny-frame glasses glide unbidden to the end of his nose. He wears the same dark suit and thin red tie to church every week.

As boys we are in awe of him. This is a man who talks of the solar system as though he has personally visited each planet and moon. He tells us that the universe is constantly expanding, that time can be measured almost as if we had a yardstick to do so, and that the faster we move the shorter we become, until we move so fast that we all but disappear. He speaks of space that bends. He tells us that everything, including ourselves, is essentially a complex system of energy, governed by internal electrical clocks. "Only you have a spirit," he adds hastily. He is a walking wonder to us. He is the first adult who allows us to call him by his first name. We don't often understand him, but we stand in awe of him. How does he know such things?

What he teaches us on Sunday often becomes grist for school friends on Monday. We feel smarter ourselves for grasping the nuggets he so easily tosses our way. To him, knowledge is exciting, knowledge is wonderful. Plus, he always has one pocket of that old black suit filled with bubble gum for us.

Bubble gum is the common currency among boys our age.

"He is brilliant," my father says. "You've heard him in Sunday School class. A first-rate intellect."

"I suppose," my mother sighs. "I'd like to press his shirts for him. He has a spot on his suit pants. I'd like to set him up with a girl some time, I just don't know who. She'd have to be awfully intelligent just to keep up a conversation with Jim. He needs a new tie. The one he wears he wore to a dinner with gravy once. At least."

All of this is about to change, and there will be no need to find a date for Jim. What changed Jim Hopson's personal universe, what set his stars and moons rolling in a different direction, what science and physics could not account for, took place when Sandy Smart walked into Sunday School opening exercises one warm, sunny Sabbath morning.

There were no student wards in those days. The college kids away from home gathered on Tuesday nights for M-Men and Gleaners, but the rest of the time, they came to a ward and were expected to fold right in. For some, especially those from the rural areas, it was a huge adjustment—big city, college, and a new ward filled with strange faces, not many of them your age.

On a Sunday morning, Sandy Smart, barely twenty years old, from a small, high-desert town called Burns, attired in her new yellow dress and white shiny shoes, walks into the chapel. Jim, now a counselor in the Sunday School presidency, sees her from his perch high above the congregation the moment she enters the room and he cannot take his eyes off her.

For the first time in his life, Jim Hopson's universe is in sudden disarray, and not even his fine intellect or any physical principle in the universe can explain to him why his world is suddenly upside down and totally out of whack.

Jim Hopson is in love.

"Amazing. She's such a cute girl. Such a sweetheart. And with the last name of Smart, and Jim being the way he is, such a brilliant mind. It is meant to be so. A match made in heaven," Mother says one evening at home, while an episode of *Gunsmoke* flickers across the television screen. "I wondered what kind of girl he might end up with and now I think I know."

"You always said you never knew what kind of a girl he'd date, but I reckon you are singing a different song, now. Yes, I'm sure Jim is fond of her," says father, watching Miss Kitty and Marshal Dillon exchange bits of wisdom at the saloon. "Very fond. I'm sure."

"She's so sweet. There is the age difference, but Jim appears younger than he is. And age isn't such a barrier. I'm much younger than you."

"Fourteen months," Father says in a monotone. "I hardly robbed the cradle."

"Wouldn't it be wonderful? He has a new blue tie, and I think he took his suit to the cleaners. He's changing. He's much more presentable. I bet he gets the door for Sandy. Love will do that to you."

"Yes, I'm sure Jim is fond of her," says Father, as Festus hobbles in, soon followed by Doc, who, as usual, is complaining about something.

"I hope it works out," Mom says.

"I hope so, too," Dad agrees.

"Wouldn't it be so right?"

Father reluctantly turns away from the chatter in the saloon and asks a question that brings Mother to a quick and complete halt.

"But does anyone know if Sandy loves him? Seems like

that's the big question here. It takes both parties to reach a suitable agreement, don't you think, Joy?"

Back in Dodge, Marshal Dillon has had enough of talk, and he pushes his way through the saloon doors, with grim determination, having decided it is high time to go after the bad guy, and if the occasion calls for it, gun him down, though he is a peaceful man by nature and reluctant to take such extreme measures. "I'd rather take him alive," he tells Miss Kitty, glancing at her over his shoulder, "but I don't know if that's possible."

Miss Kitty nods her head solemnly, her famous mole looping up and down, then calls after the marshal, "Matt, you be careful out there. You hear?"

Marshal Dillon nods seriously. "I'll be careful," he says. Then he gives Miss Kitty a wink.

It becomes one of those silent, unmistakable quests of a ward. Sometimes, it happens, say, when a beloved member is ill, and even without the prayers and updates over the pulpit, and perhaps a special ward fast, everyone knows what is happening, and the ward is unifying around a cause. It is an elevating and sometimes thrilling experience when the ward rallies round, especially when the cause is love.

And Jim Hopson and Sandy Smart became the unofficial cause and concern of the ward. Rooting for them became almost as serious a concern as fasting for a drought to end or praying for the new stake president. You could almost feel the tension when the two of them passed each other in church, and dozens of people began making mental notes and sharing them in opportune moments, which seemed just about any moment before and after church meetings, and sometimes in hushed whispers during church meetings.

Did she smile when he talked to her?

Have they gone out? They did? Where to?

Did they have a good time?

She's so young.

She wants to be a nurse. That's why she's at the university here.

Smart girl, she is. Oh, my. That's a little joke, isn't it?

He's wearing a new tie.

I hear Bishop Ranstrom wants to talk with them.

Her father is a pharmacist. The only one in the place she comes from.

Can you imagine how smart their children would be? That's a little joke, too.

She sings beautifully.

He needs a girl like that. She'll help him settle down. She'll keep his feet on the ground.

You notice they sit together at church every week now. That's a good sign.

But they don't seem too chummy, if you know what I mean.

I hear he's planning a trip to Burns over the holidays. You know what that's for.

Sounds serious to me.

Sounds serious to me, too.

I don't think she loves him.

He bought a new suit.

Maybe she loves him. I don't know. But maybe she does.

Stranger things have happened. We ended up with each other, after all, Carol.

And in the deacons quorum, we take note. The strange and churning change from boyhood to manhood is underway, our upper lips sprouting fuzz, our voices croaky. And we think we understand, though not a word escapes our lips to one another, what Jim is going through and what we hope the outcome of it all will be.

You see, we are Jim and Jim is us. Just a few years fast-forwarded.

She looks pretty in that yellow dress.

She's not that much older than we are. Not really.

I saw them holding hands after sacrament meeting last week.

That's nothing. I saw them kissing after Mutual on Tuesday.

Kissing?

Kissing. No lie. On the lips.

On the lips. That's gross. I hate it when my parents do that.

A Sunday afternoon, the first of the month. We stay after Sunday School for fast and testimony meeting. A sleepy meeting, the sunshine warm and beckoning on this unexpectedly pretty, early winter afternoon.

Members of our ward rise and bear their testimonies. Nothing unusual. My thoughts wander. I fidget. My father looks at me and shakes his head sideways, then puts his arm around me. "Not long now, amigo. Be patient."

We are sitting on the left side of the chapel. I look across the aisle, then back a couple of rows. My gaze comes to rest upon Jim Hopson. He sits next to Sandy, who looks pretty and self-conscious, in a royal blue dress, light blue cardigan sweater, and her shiny white shoes. Jim turns to look at the clock at the back of the chapel. He glances toward the ceiling, as if for inspiration. He looks down at his black shoes. He shifts his weight from side to side. He looks as though his stomach aches. All of this in the space of a half-minute. He is as restless as I am.

It does not take any particular spiritual maturity or divine insight into the human condition to know what is coming next. Even a thirteen-year-old boy can tell.

Jim Hopson is getting ready to bear his testimony.

As one speaker sits down, Jim rises and begins a swift, gawky, feverish walk toward the podium. Bishop Ranstrom's eyes lock on him and the smallest of smiles creases his face. Suddenly, a nondescript testimony meeting has evolved into something extraordinary. The eyes of the congregation are focused on Jim. An air of expectation hangs thick, heavy in the chapel.

It is as though a peal of thunder booms through the chapel, and the rain begins to fall, and everyone knows their prayers about the drought have been heard.

People expect that Jim Hopson has a message to deliver.

And deliver it he does.

Jim reaches the podium, pushes his glasses higher on his nose, squints, and runs a hand through his bushy mud-blond hair.

And in my mind, seeking some kind of telepathic miracle, I say, *Careful up there, Jim.*

He clears his throat. He says that the last few months of

his life have been special. He is thankful for his blessings. He knows the gospel is true.

Then he pauses and looks right at Sandy. And he starts talking about families, and how his fondest desire in life is to be sealed in the temple to a beautiful young woman and become a father.

Then Jim pauses and composes himself.

Sandy looks at her hands, folded in her lap, and blushes.

The entire ward hushes.

Brother Dozer snores, but Sister Dozer keeps her elbows to herself.

Bishop Ranstrom leans forward.

For some reason, I think of Marshal Dillon and his six-shooter and Miss Kitty and wonder if they were ever serious, if they dated, and what you did on a date in Dodge City anyway.

Bishop Ranstrom's eyes grow wide, then he leans over to Brother Willis, the first counselor, and whispers something in his ear. Brother Willis nods and breaks into a huge grin.

Everyone knows that Jim Hopson is going to propose over the pulpit to Sandy Smart.

And though it may not be quite an appropriate forum to do so, and though it doesn't fit into any of those general conference talks about what constitutes a true testimony, it is a sweet moment, sweet beyond belief, and yes, the Spirit does seem to be with us. Certainly, some kind of spirit is with Jim.

He begins again slowly.

"And I think I've found that beautiful young woman."

The men in the congregation are all thinking: *This is a little unusual. This is a little odd. This is a bit unorthodox. Never heard a fellow propose during his testimony. Yes, quite odd, in fact. I wonder if there's anything in the handbook on this. Should the bishop stop the meeting?*

My father looks at his black dress shoes and wiggles his toes inside of them. I can tell. The leather goes up and down, up and down.

And the sisters are all thinking: *How lovely! And he's making us a part of this. How romantic. I always thought Jim was a fine young man. My husband should take note.*

My father sits back in the pew and reaches for Mother's hand. He no longer wiggles his toes.

Jim chokes out the words. "So, Sandy, will you do me the honor of becoming my wife? I'll always take care of you, I'll always love you."

All eyes turn toward Sandy. No man, his named called from over the podium from the Tabernacle or Conference Center, and invited to take his place on one of the tall red chairs, has felt this kind of pressure, the pressure that has descended with the force of a steel slab dropped from the height of the podium on the slender shoulders of Sandy Smart.

Jim hurriedly adds, "In the name of Jesus Christ, amen," then scuttles back to his seat, eyes down, and no doubt wondering if he is the greatest fool in God's expansive universe.

Sandy sits stiffly, eyes straight ahead, her color faded from a delicate pink blush to a stark, sheer, terrible white.

The time for testimonies is over and, by all rights, Bishop Ranstrom should be rising now and saying, "Thanks to all of those who have borne their testimonies. We have all been uplifted. And now we will conclude these services by singing hymn number 290, 'Ye Simple Souls Who Stray.'"

But Bishop Ranstrom is a wise man, a man who understands timing, and he knows that an answer is coming, he knows that the moment demands more than standing up and closing the meeting. He sits steadfastly in his red chair and he, also, looks toward Sandy.

The battle of wills has begun. Bishop Ranstrom comes out on top.

Sandy rises slowly, and if they could, each member of the congregation would break into a cheer. She walks, stiff-limbed and trembling, toward the stand. The only sound in the entire chapel is the "skiff, skiff" rustling of her dress as she takes the long walk forward.

She grips both sides of the podium, lowers her head for a moment. Then she looks up and smiles radiantly, the nervousness now just a memory, and says in a clear voice, "And I think I've found my handsome young man. I accept, Jim. And I love you, too, and always will."

Murmurs and sighs and a few outright exclamations whoosh through the congregation, and our whole ward feels good. Really good. Sandy says a few testimony-like things and finishes. She walks back to the congregation. Jim stands, and when she's within reach, takes her hand and guides her to her seat.

Brother Willis slaps Bishop Ranstrom on the knee and says, loud enough for the entire ward family to hear, including those who may have been at home ill that day, "She said 'yes,' Bishop! Imagine that. Can you believe it?"

Bishop Ranstrom rises and says it was a memorable meeting, and he wants to be the first to wish the couple happiness, health, and prosperity. And then with a perfectly straight face, he looks at the chorister, Sister Foley, and says, "I think we'll change the closing hymn from 'The Wintry Day, Descending to Its Close' to hymn number 118, 'Now Let Us Rejoice.' And we had asked Brother Hopson to offer the benediction, but he's made the trip up here once already, and I'm not sure his shaky knees would carry him up here a second time, so I think we'll just have Brother Romo offer the prayer, if that's okay with everyone."

I don't suppose that it's ever the right thing to do to stand and cheer at the end of a testimony meeting, although I've had the urge to do so at the conclusion of a few that ran way, way over, but if the occasion ever neared appropriateness, this was it. Once the meeting was over, the happy young couple was fairly mobbed, the sisters all headed toward Sandy with hugging and advice on their minds and the brethren eager to pump Jim's hand and congratulate him and tell him what a fine bride Sandy will be.

"Well, it all worked out. I still can't quite believe that Jim asked her over the pulpit. God moves in mysterious ways, and sometimes, so do men," my father says on the drive home.

"It was sweet. Very sweet. Also very bizarre," Mother adds, looking out the window at the storefronts on Division Street. She pauses. "Would you have ever considered doing something like that, Hal?"

Father, perhaps feeling there was no correct answer to that question, asks me what I learned in priesthood meeting.

"We talked about Moroni," I answer.

But the lasting lesson that day came from Jim. We in the deacons quorum understood that we had been a witness to history—family history and ward history—and that this strange and glorious scene would be recounted over dinner tables for many years to come. It affected all of us, I suppose. Though Jim was more than twice our age, he seemed one of us, and if this gawky, brilliant, kind-hearted soul could capture the heart of Sandy Smart, then it gave us hope that, someday, the same thing might well happen to us. Sandy was a pretty girl. We all knew that. Maybe we'd marry a pretty girl too.

And Jim had kissed her on the lips at Mutual.

There is one thing more to add about the whole incident. As I was leaving the chapel, headed toward the parking lot, I saw Bishop Ranstrom and Brother Willis talking as they ambled down from the stand. They both wore huge smiles, and when Bishop Ranstrom spotted me, he gave me a wink.

As he did, I thought of Marshal Dillon, I thought of Jim Hopson, and I thought of Miss Kitty and Sandy Smart, and somehow, the life's star of all these people, real and imagined, seemed to intersect right where I stood, bursting into one glorious blaze, and for the first time I figured out that for all of the mysteries of the universe, all that Dr. Einstein ever thought of and theorized about, all that Moses and Enoch and Abraham understood, all that Jim knew and tried to teach us as we wiggled through our Aaronic priesthood lessons, pales by comparison with the complexity of what happens when two hearts find one another.

Marshal Dillon got his man, and yes, he had to gun him down, but not before taking one in the shoulder himself.

Doc patched him up, grumbling and cantankerous as always, and Miss Kitty came by and asked if he were okay, her mole rising in perfect synchronization with her eyebrow.

"It's nothin', Kitty. Just a flesh wound."

Nothing at all, I suppose, like being shot through the heart.

CHAPTER 9

December 1967

Robin Mitchell Hutchins comes back to live at home with her parents, Will and Sharon. Tim has been shipped overseas, to Vietnam. Robin is expecting their first child, due any time. Her husband will not be with her when she delivers the baby. So Robin has come home.

The week before Christmas, and the conditions in Portland are ripe for a snowstorm. Bitter cold air from Canada slides down the west side of the Cascade Mountains and mixes with a wet storm front sailing in from the Pacific. It begins to snow on a Thursday and continues all day. At noon, we are sent home from school. Then the east wind howls up the Columbia River Gorge and the snow begins to drift. Portland seldom sees much snow, but this storm is a doozy.

In the middle of the night, somewhere between Friday and Saturday, with drifts two feet deep and snow still blowing sideways across the landscape and the wind making a noise like I've never heard before—low, rumbling, threatening, like an animal that is hurt—the snow begins to find its way under our front door and into our living room. I lie awake and listen to the blowing snow pelting against the windows and think it sounds more like a desert sandstorm than a blizzard.

All this, and Sharon Mitchell calls a little after midnight and says, "Robin is in labor. Her water broke. She's going fast. Will's so sick he can't even sit up in bed. Can you drive her to the hospital, Hal? She said she'd feel comfortable with you."

My father yawns and raises his arms above his head and then rubs his eyes, and his voice is as calm as pond water.

"Why, sure. Be right over. Tell Robin not to worry. Let me put some heavy clothes on."

As far back as I can remember, Father has served as the ward financial clerk, the stake financial clerk, and as the elders quorum instructor. Then he and mother get called into the stake president's office one night, and on the following Sunday, he is sustained as the second counselor to Bishop Ranstrom when Brother Romo is released. Father is in his mid-forties and is ordained a high priest by Bishop Ranstrom before being set apart.

"It'll be nice to work with Bishop Ranstrom," says Father. "He's a good man and a good bishop, and I reckon we'll get along just fine."

That's about all he ever said to us regarding his calling. He never even mentioned his new calling before being sustained. We learned about it when the ward learned about it. No star treatment for him. And with that, he simply went to work.

"Neal, are you awake?"

"Yes. I heard the phone ring. Is everything okay?"

"Well, yes, it's okay, but Robin needs our help. She's going to have a baby. Will's sick and can't get her to the hospital. The weather's bad. I think freezing rain has started."

"Do you want me to come?"

"I do. Sharon's coming, and she'll tend to Robin. But if we slide off the road or get stuck in a drift, I'd like you along. We could put your muscles to good use."

"Sure, Dad. Let me get dressed. Let's go. Robin's baby. Wow."

That same month, Dad's first of conducting sacrament meeting, Bishop Ranstrom asked Father to arrange the speakers.

"Anyone special for the Sunday before Christmas?"

"No, I'll leave that up to you, Hal. You've been in the ward as long as I have."

"I think I know who."

Freezing rain drops icy pellets from the night sky, coating everything in a slick glaze. By comparison, snow would have been a pleasure to drive in. I hear the plink-plink-plink of the rain hitting my bedroom window as I hurriedly throw on a warm shirt, gloves, my heaviest pants, and my winter coat.

"Who is going to speak at the Christmas sacrament meeting, Hal? I heard you say that Bishop Ranstrom asked you to take care of that."

"Well, Joy, I'm thinking of someone you'd probably never guess. I think he's the one. You know, you want someone special for this sacrament meeting, somebody who can talk a little about life as well as Christmas."

Mother ticks off a few names—a former stake president, a past beloved bishop, a couple of others known for their oratorical skills. Father smiles and shakes his head. "None of them."

"Well, who then, Hal? That about exhausts my list."

"Who? Well, I asked him last night. He didn't want to. It took some coaxing because he's not much of a talker. But I asked Robert Blue."

The surprise is evident in Mother's voice. "Robert Blue?"

I push away the screen door and walk to the driveway where Dad is in the car. My foot hits the icy pavement, and the next thing I know, I am sliding down our driveway and toward the street on this frictionless surface. Somehow, I manage to dig my heels and fingertips into the ice and slow my slide, but not until I have glided out into the street. Father gets out of the car and laughs and says, "Got your baseball shoes nearby?"

"In the garage, I think."

"Better put them on. The cleats will give you traction."

Brother Blue has been in our ward for about five years. He is short, thickly built, frizzy-haired, quiet. My impressions of him come from snatches of conversation I have heard from my parents and other adults.

Tough luck, Robert has had.

Too bad about his wife. She's never been quite healthy. Thought the surgery might fix things up. Guess it didn't.

Never says much. Doesn't have much to say, I guess. Quiet fellow.

He was a school custodian. Not sure what he's doing now. Don't know much about him.

His kids are nice. Real nice kids, but they don't talk much either. What's he got? Two boys and a little girl?

Brother Blue never misses on home teaching. One hundred percent, regular as clockwork.

He's about the first one to show up when someone needs help moving.

Helped me take down a tree when the wind knocked it over.

I think things might be tough at his house.

I think Brother Blue is a good man.

We carefully inch our way up the stairs to the Mitchells' front door. Before we can knock, Mrs. Mitchell leads her daughter gingerly out onto the porch. Robin is wearing a heavy coat and thick socks and carries a small bag. Before stepping onto the porch she pauses for a moment, her face reflecting a pain she is having. When she sees me, she smiles tiredly and says, "Oh, Neal. I'm sorry to pull you out on a night like this."

Father says, "Okay, Sharon, I'll have Neal here walk with you to the car. He's got on his baseball shoes so his footing will be good. Robin, I want you to throw your arm around my shoulder and put your other hand on my arm. We'll be fine. Quite an adventure. Won't this be a good story to tell someday?"

And with that, we walk, a pair of cautious twosomes, across the glassy sheet of ice, bundled against the chipping and nicking of the freezing rain, toward the car, its motor running, heater blasting, the east wind screaming in our ears. My cleats holding fast on the slippery surface.

"Brother Blue has something to say. He is a man of experience," Father says. "Sometimes, when nothing goes right, you feel as though you are nothing. Sometimes, when you are quiet, it's the time you need to be asked to speak. Sometimes," my father says, "what the quiet man or quiet woman has to say is exactly what we need to hear."

The drive to the hospital is accomplished by inches and feet, not blocks or miles. The speedometer shows that we are not even making five miles an hour. I sit next to father in the front seat, with Mrs. Mitchell and Robin in the backseat. Every so often, Robin moans and shifts, and once, when I look back, in the dimness of the early morning hour, I see tears wandering down her face.

"It's okay, baby, it's okay. We're getting closer now," Mrs. Mitchell soothes.

Father is a picture of concentration, feeling what little

traction there is on the tires through the steering wheel, hunched over, studying the section of the glassy road ahead illuminated by our headlights.

"How are we doing?" he occasionally asks.

"Okay," Robin says. "I'm sorry."

"When I called the ambulance, they said they couldn't guarantee arriving within two hours," Mrs. Mitchell says. "Not good enough. Not sure we have two hours."

"We're fine," my father says. "We're making good progress. What a story we'll have to tell. How are you doing back there, Robin?"

"I hurt. I'm sorry. I hurt."

Brother Blue sits stiffly on the stand, just to my father's left. He has on a well-worn gray suit, a red tie, and a red handkerchief tucked into the breast pocket of his jacket. His eyes seem locked on the back of the chapel, perhaps on the painting of the Savior, staff in one hand, a lamb in His other. He grips his typewritten talk with stiff fingers. He looks as though he is in pain.

Our front wheels slide and the back of the car fishtails. Father takes his foot off the accelerator. The car does a slow-motion pirouette in the middle of a deserted street, sliding in a wide arc, narrowly missing a vehicle parked on the side of the road, skimming by a stop sign and through a red light and out of an intersection, before coming to a rest against a snow bank. Father looks toward Mrs. Mitchell and

Robin. "Just to make things interesting. Another part of the good story. Look at this. The car is pointed in just the right direction. Let's get you to the hospital now. We're good. We're good." And he eases the Oldsmobile back onto the icy road.

The sacrament is done. The carols have been sung, melodic numbers by our choir. It is time for the Christmas speaker. The chapel is full. Brother Blue rises from his chair. Then he slowly twirls back to his chair and stiffly reaches to the floor for his scriptures. He takes three tiny, tentative steps and places his scriptures and his talk on the podium. He looks pale and he trembles. He clears his throat. And then he begins.

"There really is only one Christmas story to tell. 'And it came to pass in those days, that there went out a decree from Caesar Augustus . . . '"

"Just a few minutes more and we'll be there. Hal will get us through. He will. Almost there, baby. It's okay, Robin, it's okay, it's okay."

Brother Blue tells us the Christmas story. He recites from Luke. He never looks down. Then he says he has always loved stories told from the pulpit. So he begins again. He tells us stories. He tells us his Christmas stories, our Brother Blue. He tells of Christmases long ago, growing up on a ranch in northern Wyoming. He tells of Christmases in the mission field. He tells of times when he gave at Christmas even though he had little to give.

I didn't know that he had served a mission.

A lovely, hushed enchantment settles on our congregation. This is a good simple man, telling good simple Christmas stories, stories that are true, and with each passing moment, his confidence grows, the gentle humor shines, and the things he has learned from his experiences are generously given to us.

A gift, from Brother Blue.

To all of us.

On the second row of the chapel, Sister Blue looks serene and their children attentive. They are thinking, *That is my husband speaking on Christmas Day*, and, *My father is someone or he would not be speaking on Christmas Day.*

Robin's pain mounts, and she lets out a sharp yelp and calls for her husband, Tim, and she buries her head into her mother's shoulder and grips her mother's wrist so hard that Mrs. Mitchell once says, "Robin, you need to loosen up a bit. My arm is asleep."

At last, through the sheet of freezing rain, we see the hospital and the red block letters that say "EMERGENCY." Father pulls as close to the door as he can and then says to me, "Neal, run in and tell them there is a young woman who is about to deliver a baby any minute. They'll get out here as soon as you say that."

And they do. A flurry and bustle of nurses and a young doctor somehow defy the laws of physics and run to the car and get Robin into a wheelchair and whisk her through the doors. I see Robin, who used to read me bedtime stories, someone who told me where to hide and when to run and what to watch out for when we played games on summer evenings. Her face is pale and, despite the cold, she is perspiring. She says once more she's sorry, then she grimaces and is gone. Not far behind is Mrs. Mitchell. Father and I stand next to the idling car, the freezing rain digging and biting into our faces.

"Guess that's it," my father says. "She'll be fine."

"Guess so."

"Best idea I've had in a long time, getting you to grab those baseball shoes. You got right up to the entrance."

"They helped."

"Should we go home now?"

I thought for a moment. It didn't feel like our business was quite finished.

"Can we stay?"

"Oh, I think we can. It's Saturday, though, isn't it? No work and you wouldn't go to school today anyway. I'll find a place to park and then we'll go to the waiting room. I don't think Robin and Sharon will mind. I'm kind of interested in seeing how this all works out anyway. Quite a night we've had. Quite a night. I was glad for your company."

From the waiting room, we called my mother and told her not to worry, that we'd made it safely. Father and I did our fair share of pacing, and we saw a couple of fathers age several years in the space of two hours, walking back and forth, jumping a foot into the air whenever anyone pushed through the big doors from the delivery rooms. We watched them smile and shout and instantly adopt us as brothers when the good news came. Father and I got some watery cocoa from a machine, tried to talk a little baseball, and maybe dozed just a bit.

It was first light, just a faint gray to the east, when Mrs. Mitchell wearily shuffled into the waiting room, smiled at both of us, and said, "A boy. He's healthy and doing fine. So is Robin. Thank you. Thank you so much." And then she sat down and burst into tears.

At the end of the meeting, I saw many people walk up to Brother Blue and congratulate him on his talk. I saw many of our ward members do the same to Sister Blue and their children. Last among them was my father, who warmly shook Robert Blue's hand and said, "You have proven that wise men are still a part of Christmas."

A little more than a week later, I listened as my father talked to Robert Blue on the telephone.

"It's a start," he said. "It's not a great wage, but you can provide for your family on it. I'm proof of that. The fellow just gave his notice, so you'd start in two weeks. . . . We'd sure love to have you down at the box plant, Robert. You're good with your hands. I've seen you work on the new stake center. You can stop by tomorrow and see me and fill out the papers. . . . Okay? . . . Good. . . . About nine o'clock would be best for me."

Father, it seems, is going to teach someone else about boxmaking.

And a year later, after Tim Hutchins got back from

Vietnam, I saw Tim and Robin get out of a car in front of the Mitchells' house. I saw Tim take his son, Timothy Neal Hutchins, in his arms and walk with the pride of a new father to the doorway. I saw the door open at the Mitchells' home, heard the exultant cries, witnessed the storm of arms flying and magically transforming into hugs.

It was a good story and now it had a good ending.

What to make of that memorable December? This: The birth of a baby boy, and all that can be said about that; the rebirth of a wise man at a time of year when the greatest present to him was a simple gift of hope, and his gift back to us, simple wisdom, which all wisdom is.

Robert Blue worked at the box plant for more than ten years.

And three summers later, just before I left for my freshman year in college, a tow-haired little boy and I played baseball with a plastic ball and bat in the Mitchells' front yard.

I wanted to tell him that I was there when he was born, but I didn't. So instead I told him, when you have two strikes on you, choke up on the bat. It makes it easier to hit the ball.

I don't think he understood what I meant.

Someday, he will.

CHAPTER 10

April 1963

Sometimes, from nowhere, I remember a talk, a look, a warm feeling that flies to me from my growing years. It's all there, I think, all that experience. It comes back to us, filtered by age, and if we're lucky, wisdom, and we make and take a meaning from it. We understand better why people acted the way they did, what was behind their words. Experience is a window, if we'll take the time to look and see what we can see.

Nowhere did I have a better window than the first two pews on the south side of our chapel. The benches didn't face directly forward but were slightly angled toward the pulpit and the congregation. It is where the deacons sat, twice on most Sundays, readying themselves to pass the sacrament. It was our place. It was a time before young men were excused, their priesthood honor and obligation fulfilled, to return to sit with their families. We sat in the same place, through the rest of the meeting, beyond the reach of parents. The two rows were the deacons' home for Sunday School and sacrament meeting. From these rows, our bodies turned slightly to the left, we had a perfect view of the congregation and the stand. These rows were our perch. We could see almost everything from there, a perfect angle of vision for the entire chapel, and because we were out of the line of sight of the rest of the congregation, we may have seen more than anyone, even the bishopric.

We knew what was going on in the ward. We saw the little stories, the little incidents, that took place each Sabbath day. We felt like spies.

The people, the people of this old ward, gathered in that old graceful building. I remember them clearly, the indelible marks they left upon me, most, I think, without ever suspecting their influence.

There was the appropriately named Brother Dozer, beetle-browed, floppy-eared, multiple-chinned, with a large, happy face, who invariably fell asleep during sacrament meeting. When he would drift off to sweet slumber and begin to snore, he would be awakened by a quick, darting elbow from Sister Dozer, a thin, sober woman. After feeling the sting of his wife's elbow, Brother Dozer would always sit up with a start and often mumble, "Fine talk, fine talk. That brother knows his stuff, amen," before usually drifting off to sleep again within minutes.

There was the Granger family, always on the third row, the ten children sitting in ascending order, according to age. Brother Granger had been in the military for many years, a colonel in the army. He was a man who enjoyed order, a taste that carried to where his family sat on Sundays and the arrangement of his children on the pew, all sitting with backs straight, eyes to the front, hands on laps. Diminutive Sister Granger, as far as I can remember, even with ten children, hardly ever raised her voice above a whisper. Perhaps it was all coping, a way to keep her sanity, in the midst of finely tuned chaos.

And there was Sister Brooks, the bony-faced ward chorister—vibrant and dramatic, bleached-blonde hair curled and stacked high upon her head, jewelry clinking, arms held wide and expressive as she directed the singing, her thin, white baton flying in looping arcs, large motions, and sharp, quick cuts. Sister Brooks, my father used to say, reminded him of a helicopter getting ready to take off, a comment that invariably drew a "Now, Hal . . ." caution from Mother.

"Someday," Father countered with assuredness, "she will take off as she leads the singing. She will fly right out of the chapel, out into the clear blue sky, and it will be retold through the ages as the Miracle of Sister Brooks. Mark my words. I said it first."

From the deacons' perch, we could also see the loose-jointed, jaunty Brother Parker, the funniest man I've known in my life, who always carried a package of mints and was known to have a soft spot in his heart for deacons, perhaps because he was one of us in most ways excepting age.

From our designated place, we could see when the bishopric leaned over and quietly conversed with one another, when they passed notes. We could see their fingers drumming on their knees when a speaker went on too long and the worried glances they cast toward a certain family or ward member when something wasn't quite right. We could tell, by the slightest change in his otherwise stoic face, when something was said that made Bishop Ranstrom uncomfortable. We could see, too, when a speaker droned on, and it was a warm evening, and the songbirds outside chirped as the sun slid toward the dark green West Hills, the times when he let go and seemed to enjoy just sitting, the weight of responsibility shifted away from his strong shoulders for a few minutes. We could see him flinch and wince when a soloist tried mightily to hit a note and missed it.

On those hard, wood pews, before the day when cushions were laid down upon them, we had a sideways view of those who were about to speak—from the calm and self-assured to those whose knees trembled, shoulders slumped, heads continually screening the congregation from side to side. We could see the brother who mopped beads of perspiration from his forehead before beginning his talk, the sister who carefully dabbed tissue. We could see them, when their talks were over, lifted and light and relieved as they gratefully slumped back into one of the comfortable red chairs.

And we were only a few feet from white-haired Brother Swanson when he suddenly slumped over during a fast meeting, and we saw the horrified, panic-stricken look on his wife's face, her hand in the air motioning. We could hear the whoosh of air from Brother Wagner, a fireman, as he breathed life back into Brother Swanson, and all the while Sister Pearson continued to bear her testimony, with remarkable poise and purpose, though she was acutely aware of the drama taking place in the front-left part of the chapel, no more than twenty feet away from her.

This was our place, our observation point, where we observed much of life—human beings at their finest, godlike at their best moments. We saw them all and as deacons, if we paid attention, we learned about faith and strength and humility and courage, not to mention the varied condition and nature of humankind. And besides, it was fun and broke up the meeting for us.

Quite a window it was.

Everyone should sit near the front of the chapel, off to the side, and be able to watch the congregation unfettered. I think we would be a more understanding people.

Memories on every row, memories from every Sunday as I grew up, and while many of the lessons we were taught in class ebb and fade and fall into blank memory, the lessons we learned just by watching have endured.

It was all cozy, familiar, inviting, and warm. It was a good place to be—in church. Outside, the storms may have raged, but inside, all was as it should be.

I see her. She stands stately in front of the congregation, Sunday mornings. Sunday School opening exercises. Light shines through the pane glass windows.

There is the organ, solemn, deep, its bass notes resembling distant thunder, the pipes above it thin and reedy. They look like little long faces, the organ pipes. Their vents look like mouths and eyes, a tall and thin wind-blown choir.

Sister Palmer rises, a slim baton in her right hand, the blue hymn book in her left, and walks the few short steps from her seat on the stand to a small platform in front of the organ. She opens the hymnbook, she finds the page, she listens to the organ finish the introduction, and she raises the baton. Unlike Sister Brooks', her counterpart in sacrament meeting, Sister Palmer's motion is compact and plain.

The singing begins:

> Jesus of Nazareth,
> Savior and King!
> Triumphant over death,
> Life thou didst bring.

The volume of the singing rises a little and becomes more thoughtful. This is worship, it is worship we feel in our ward at this time, with the bright light from the leaded window flowing in, Sister Palmer leading the music, the organ both solemn and sweet.

Bishop Ranstrom looks toward the priests, who rise from their seats and pull back the sacrament table cloth and begin to break bread.

On our row, we deacons sit still and look ahead and then look at Sister Palmer.

> Leaving thy Father's throne,
> On earth to live.

And the tears begin to fall down Sister Palmer's face.

It was the tears. It was the tears that we noticed. Sister Palmer was someone we did not know well. She lived alone. Forty years old, I would guess. My mother once said she had a good job. People sometimes talked about a sadness, a tragedy in her life. We didn't know what it was. Was she thinking of this tragedy when she led the sacrament hymn during Sunday School? Is that what caused the tears?

She was forty and she lived alone and she wept when the sacrament song was sung. And I longed to learn more of the mystery of Sister Palmer—what secrets she kept, her aura of composure and calm, outlined by an unknown sadness.

Or so I thought, as a young boy.

We wondered. We wondered among ourselves, and sometimes, we wondered with each other. A deacon new to our ward, new to Sister Palmer, once tried to make fun of her.

"She cries, she always cries," he said, as though we had never noticed. "She's some kind of baby, that's what I think," he said. "A crybaby."

We didn't pay attention to him. And our silence conveyed a message that talking about Sister Palmer was out of bounds. He never said anything about her tears again. No teasing. No speculation, unless it was grounded in honest thought and question. Sister Palmer, even to a bunch of ragtag deacons, was too dignified. Why she cried, we knew, must be important. Maybe it was the tragedy. We sat at the front of the chapel. We knew the ward, we knew everything that went on. Or so we thought. Except for one thing: why Sister Palmer cried.

> Thy work to do alone,
> Thy life to give.

The tears didn't gush and run down her cheeks. They were small, there were only a few, they were delicate. Did she go home at night and think to herself that she wished she wouldn't cry? Did she say to herself, I will not weep when I lead the music for the sacrament hymn? Or did she just know that it would never be another way for her?

She sang alto, deeper than what you would think from someone of her size and bearing. A low, steady, calm singing voice.

> We'll sing all hail to Jesus' name,
> And praise and honor give . . .

"Sister Palmer is a wonderful woman," my father says, "kind and sweet and very talented in music."

We are at my Great-uncle Rich's property, in his apple orchard that slopes away from his house. It is a late April day, raw and windy, the heavy cumulus clouds crawling over the Coast Range to the west, rumbling our way.

Uncle Rich's orchard needs pruning. Sucker branches on the tree limbs stand as straight and tall as tin soldiers, and they must be trimmed. "Apple tree branches need to look as though they are reaching down to the earth, not upward to the sky," my father tells me. Uncle Rich, now in his mid-seventies, can no longer prune the apple trees on his five acres, so father and I have come to help, as we have for the last couple of years. Our reward for doing so is all the sweet and crispy Golden Delicious apples our family can carry away when harvest comes in September. Uncle Rich, dressed in a heavy cotton shirt and overalls, green rubber boots, and an old, fleecy brown jacket, walks among his trees and thanks us again and again.

"Hate to give up on these trees. They're good producers. Someone always can use apples," he says. "Cold enough out here to be December, though. When you're done, we'll go back up to the house and get some cocoa."

All around his home and orchard, others sell their apples in the fall. Uncle Rich has always just given his away. Father said Uncle Rich started doing so during the Depression, when times were difficult in the 1930s.

"For all we know, these trees made the difference in people getting through," Father said to me on our drive out. "Rich's name is respected here. Respected a lot by different folks because of the kind of man he is. Whatever he had, he gave of it, never asked anything in return."

With long, powerful strokes, Father trims a straight tree limb off, the saw making a pleasant, rhythmical zoo-zaw sound.

"Looks ugly now, but if you want a bushy tree that doesn't produce apples, you let it go," Uncle Rich explains, "You've got to prune. These little trees don't know it, but you're doing them a favor. They're nothing but pretty to look at in the spring if you don't trim 'em."

"Rain is coming," my father says. "So cold it almost feels like snow. Wind's kicking up. You're right, Rich. Feels more like December. If we were smarter, we'd be inside right now."

"Well, just goes to show we aren't all that smart, Hal. Tell me again. What happened to the Palmer girl? Ed's daughter?"

Uncle Rich occasionally visits our ward. He knew Edward Palmer, Sister Palmer's father. He asks about Sister Palmer every time we prune, every time we come to his home for

Easter dinner. That's the kind of man he is, an endless curiosity about the well-being of others.

"Just the same. Still works. No marriage prospects, as far as I know," Father says. And he repeats, "Talented woman. Very sweet. The why of her life, I just don't get, but I suppose it's not my worry. I don't know the whys of many lives, hardly my own. But you should hear her sing."

Uncle Rich says, "I have. She's an alto. Beautiful voice. Didn't get that from her father, though. Ed couldn't sing any more than rocks in a bucket."

Father says, "Too bad about that fellow. Not her dad, Ed, but the other fellow."

Uncle Rich says, "Yes. Two weeks before they were going to get married. He never knew what hit him, I guess. I hope. It's a shame, though. Surely is."

The cold rain starts, drops coming straight down, no wind driving it. I gather up another armload of pruned branches and drop them onto a growing pile.

We work for another hour. Father sawing, Uncle Rich snipping off the smaller suckers, me gathering and piling. The rain turns steady and stings my face. The Coast Range disappears as the clouds lumber inland, and overhead, the cumulus clouds lower. Soon enough, the tops of the tall Douglas fir trees across the road from Uncle Rich's house are shrouded in mist. This rain is setting in, as it can only do in the Pacific Northwest. Damp to the bone, chilly, incessant.

"You're doing a fine job, Neal," says Uncle Rich.

I throw more limbs into a pile. A robin sings its three-note rain song. The rainwater seeps underneath my coat, down inside my shirt. My wet trousers are plastered to my skin. I shiver and look up to see my father's eyes on me.

"Think it's about time? We're soaked, and I better be getting Neal home," he says.

"Yes, it's time. Let's get that cocoa before you get on your way. Thanks, gentlemen. It'll help."

Uncle Rich tramps his foot down on the last pile I made. To no one in particular, he says, "She sings so well. She sings pretty. I think she's a nice gal, too."

Last Saturday, it was cloudy but dry. We played baseball in the street. A couple of the dads came out to watch us. Sam Tuller was pitching, and he lobbed one right over, belt-high, and I hit it a mile, past the telephone pole, which doubled as our home run line. It dribbled all the way to the end of the street, onto 36th Avenue. I ran around the bases slowly, listening to the chorus of approvals from the fathers who were watching. *Looks like a ballplayer, they said. Nice hit, Neal. You smacked it.*

Last week, I was playing baseball at this time. This week, I am shivering in a car after helping my great uncle in his orchard. There will be other baseball games and other long hits. The apples in the orchard will be ready in September.

After the break for cocoa, Uncle Rich walks with us to the car, in the slant-rainstorm, his thick-soled green rubber boots leaving indentations in the mud. He thanks us again and invites us to come back in the fall, when the apples are yellow-gold and crisp. He claps me on the shoulder as I get into the car and says, "You've done the work of a man today, Neal."

The trip home. Car keys jangling, a gauzy warmth in my stomach, remnants of the hearty hot chocolate Aunt Lorene fixed. The wipers swish back and forth across the windshield. Warm air blows obligingly from the heater vents on our 1959 Oldsmobile. Father's hands on the enormous steering wheel, guiding the car down wet roads. Our clothes smell of dampness, of sweat and rain together, pungent but not disagreeable. I have done a man's work this day, Uncle Rich said so, maybe the first time in my life I can make that claim. My hands are pale and wrinkled from the hard labor of the day.

Now, in the flat gray of a rainy Saturday afternoon, I feel drowsy. My head tilts back, but before I fall into a blissful dark sleep, a scrap of conversation roars into my consciousness, the thought comes into my mind, quick like lightning, and the question tumbles out, then hangs for a moment in the warm, comfortable air.

"Dad, why does she cry in Sunday School? You and Uncle Rich talked about her. I just wondered. She cries when she sings, but I wondered why she cries."

The windshield wipers go back and forth, back and forth, in wide long arcs. The water from the rain comes, the water from the rain goes. It gets shoved aside, moved away, and for an instant, the curved plate of glass is free from the tracks of rainwater.

I see the windshield and I see the water and I think of Sister Palmer and the way she weeps and whether there is a way for her to have her tears wiped away.

Father keeps his grip on the wheel and stares straight ahead, into the gathering gloom, into the rain, driving straight ahead. He says, "I could answer, I could tell you why, at least what I think, but it's something that I believe will be better for you to learn yourself. It will mean more to you and you will understand it at once and you will never forget."

He pauses, then says, "We'll go back to Rich's in the fall and pick some apples."

And with that, the abrupt change in conversation, I know, for now, the talk has ended and my father will say no more on the subject of Karen Palmer.

The windshield is glazed by rain and then it is wiped clean. The windshield is glazed by rain and then it is wiped clean. Again and again.

I roll my head comfortably upon my father's shoulder and close my eyes and let the mellowness of sleep borne of hard work overtake me, a mystery remaining a mystery, until some other day and time.

Eight years later, I sit in a small chapel in a small town off one of the main highways of Mississippi. I wear a suit and a white shirt and a missionary name tag. Outside, the weather is suffocating. The shirt-wringing humidity is nearly unbearable, and the heat that started in the eighties at sunrise has been making its slow, lazy way up the thermometer ever since.

To my left is Elder Jackson. To my right is Mrs. Devereaux and her fourteen-year-old daughter. We met them the week before, in the most difficult of all ways for missionaries to meet anyone: knocking doors, on a sickly, pale, stifling

Mississippi afternoon. Maybe it was the heat and the thought that these two poor boys in their suits, light-eyed and parched, could use something cool to drink; maybe it was because Mrs. Devereaux had a son about our age, living far from home. Maybe it was both, combined with something far more subtle that had its seeds in a masterful plan, before the division of light, before earth was created, before we took form, before we came to this world, before we had a heavy dark curtain draped across our minds and were sent forth to be tested. Maybe it was simply the gravity of a great and subtle plan that touched, took hold, and would not let go.

Mrs. Devereaux and her daughter, Jamie, had been taught the first two discussions and accepted our invitation to attend our small branch, where the branch president, a man with a high forehead, coal-black hair slicked straight back, a man who worked in a lumberyard, and whose sense of peace about everything around him I still envy today, stood up and began the services with a deep-voiced, comfortable, thick-as-good-grits accent, "Mornin', y'all, and welcome to our little church."

And as a missionary, at a moment like that, you hope. You hope that the branch members will be friendly, that the prayers will be simple and earnest, that the speakers will be true. You hope that the Spirit is there, as unmistakable and powerful as the consuming heat, the straight Mississippi pines, the encompassing humidity. All of these things you hope, and more, not understanding, at that young age, the need to simply trust and let that form of spiritual gravity take over.

You hope all those things, and you hope them so hard that it makes your body ache, and everything about you, for good and bad, is accentuated, and you would do almost anything to ensure the people sitting next to you feel what you feel and understand that it is their breathtaking privilege to have a member of the Godhead sway them gently. And it is all happening in a small chapel in the Mississippi pine-and-hill country on a white-hot day in July.

And from the stand, the branch president smiles at you and gives you the thumbs-up sign.

The prelude to the sacrament hymn begins. A slender lady stands in front of the small group and raises her hand to lead the singing. She wears thick, dark-rimmed glasses, a pink cotton dress. She is not much older than I am. I see her husband on the pew in front of us, with their two small daughters, also in pink dresses. Why is it that the sight of a mother and her two young daughters, all dressed in look-alike dresses and old, well-polished shoes, speaks to me as much as any sermon I have heard? The sweetness of it all. The sweetness of it then. She raises her hand, and the piano, not an organ, vibrates clear notes to the sky. She sings, a pleasant alto voice, hymn number 263.

> He died! The Great Redeemer died,
> And Israel's daughters wept around.

Her voice, her voice. I think of Sister Palmer, and an image of tears and water on a windshield come back to me as vividly as the stifling Mississippi heat—heat that you can see, heat like the color of lightning, heat that makes pine trees droop and strong men pass out.

A solemn darkness veiled the sky;
A sudden trembling shook the ground.

The young song leader in front of me. Her eyes moisten, a tear, lovely as a pearl, delicate as a dewdrop, rolls down her left cheek. Israel's daughters weep yet today.

To my side, I look at Mrs. Devereaux, and her eyes are fixed on this young sister, the mother of two, her neat, worn pink dress, her right hand moving rhythmically in the air. What she sees is what she needs to know. All she needs to know. Mrs. Devereaux is transfixed.

These are not tears of sorrow. They are tears of joy and appreciation.

The windshield of the car is glazed with water and the water is swept away.

***

We went back that fall and gathered apples, and Uncle Rich again asked about Sister Palmer. Uncle Rich, that's the kind of man he was.

He also said, "Here's a couple of boxes of apples. Extra. Just give 'em away to someone you think could use 'em."

My dad said he had a home teaching family or two who would like them.

It was a clear day, bright, almost cold enough for the first frost. There was no rain. There were no tears.

***

And my father was right: When I found out, when I understood why it was that Sister Palmer wept, it meant far more to me than if I had been told, if someone had supposed to tell me their interpretation of what occurred when the sacrament song was being played and sung in Sunday School and Sister Palmer rose gracefully to lead us in worship.

And worship it was. Pure worship, the way sacrament meeting should aim to be each Sabbath.

More than a year later, when I am about to leave the mission field and return to Oregon, I stop by the Devereauxes' home and ask, "What was it? When was the moment?"

Sister Devereaux said, "When I saw the young woman weep at the words to the song, I knew I had found my spiritual home. I knew who you worshiped and how, and the feelings that you told us would come came then. It was that. Only that. Nothing more. Through a song."

Windows are glazed with water and then the water is wiped away. Our lives are glazed with tears and then the tears are wiped away

After my mission, I heard that Sister Palmer had married a widower in California, moved away, and was helping to raise three daughters. My father said she was doing well. He said he was glad because she deserved as much. He always loved people who tried.

Then he looked at me, this gentle boxmaker, and said, "Do you know why now, Neal? Do you remember the apples at Uncle Rich's and how it rained on the way back?"

I said, "Yes, I know why now." I said that the tears were different from the rain. I said the rain always went away, there was a place for it to go. The tears, I said, were a tribute and they were good tears.

He looked satisfied and said I was right and then he said, "Say, do you remember that the apples we got from Uncle Rich's orchard that fall were the best we ever tasted? Sweet, so natural." He added that when he thought about it, the fact that we lived in a world where apple trees could grow at all and produce fruit was nothing short of a miracle.

A miracle. "That we have apples is a miracle," he repeated.

Best apples he'd ever eaten. He said it was because the trees were pruned just right.

I understood enough to know that he wasn't really talking about apples at all.

CHAPTER 11

May 1967

R obin Mitchell's wedding was the first among those of our generation, but it certainly was not the last. Within a few years, we saw the Martino boys and the Tullers' girl and the son and daughter of the Baileys all march off to matrimony. I had two pretty, older sisters, Maggie and Claire. It was inevitable. Someday, boys would begin paying attention to them also, and they would, against all the good-natured warnings of my father, begin to pay attention to boys. It was only a matter of time before Father would be introduced to a young man and have to ask him serious, difficult questions, and then give away his daughter to someone he barely knows and may not even like all that much. And my sister and her newfound boyfriend, based on what will seem like a quick and superficial relationship, would make commitments calculated to last through the eternities.

As a boy, I went to many wedding receptions in our ward building. The layout made it a perfect setting:

As you approached the Harrison Street building, you ascended a flight of stone stairs to the front entrance where a set of wooden double-doors opened to twelve, maroon-carpeted steps that led up to the rear of the chapel. If you walked past the raised-relief wood wall and the back row of pews, you came to a set of smaller double doors fashioned of wood and you would find yourself in what we always called "the lounge," a small room featuring a pale white-and-gray marbled fireplace. There was just enough room for a family to stand in front of the fireplace, to pose for photographs, and to receive the long line of well-wishers who happily filed through. It was a perfect spot, the right place, for a bride and groom to stand and meet the world as husband-and-wife for the first time.

———

"So he's coming home with you?" My father cannot disguise the tone of surprise in his voice, the timbre of concern.

On the other end of the line, my eldest sister, Maggie, is on the phone, calling from faraway Utah.

"I see," Father murmurs, and he senses, no doubt, his world beginning to wobble and shudder and about to veer into an entirely new galaxy. "I will"—and here he clears his throat, and I think his voice sounds distant and somehow strained—"I will look forward to meeting him and welcoming him . . . him. Him to our home. You say his name is Larry? And he is from where?"

Mother has walked into the room and, with well-honed maternal insight, she senses the significance of this moment.

She asks, "Who is Daddy talking to?"

"To Maggie. She's coming home with someone," my younger brother says.

"I'm not sure Father is happy about it," says Rosie, my youngest sister. "The way he's talking. I don't think he's happy."

"His name is Larry. That's who is coming home with Maggie," I say.

"Larry? We haven't heard much of him. I suppose we will hear much more in a very short time," Mother says. "Larry. I wonder what his last name is."

Days slide by. May slips into June. The Oregon rose bushes burst into bloom and the rhododendrons begin to bud. Young conifer trees sport their new, fresh, pale-green growth, their new needles soft and supple. The Pacific rains become less frequent. The earth turns on its huge, strong axis, and summer sweeps our way. Maggie will be home from college in two weeks. She will drive home with Larry, this stranger, Larry.

Father becomes distant as her arrival approaches. He takes walks, and he spends time alone in our small basement. Then he shows up at home from work one afternoon a little after two. "Just felt like it," he says. "Just wanted to come home." Father *never* came home early from the box plant.

He spends long hours in the yard, fertilizing the lawn, trimming the shrubbery, and working in the flowerbeds. He takes brush and bucket to places where winter has chipped away the white paint from our home. Sometimes, he just stops and stares to the east, the direction from which Maggie will come.

My father broods. Once, I see him in his favorite chair, family photo album open, staring at a picture of Maggie.

I ask Mother, "Is he all right?"

She says, "He is all right. Don't worry, Neal. He is all right."

"When will Maggie be home?"

"Shortly. A week from Thursday. She'll be at home for a while."

"Is Dad sick?"

"No, he is not sick. He is a dad. He's being a dad. You'll understand someday."

Father works more furiously in the yard. The lawn is edged, the beds are weeded. He applies more fertilizer to the grass, and a week later, the new mown grass is a lush, deep green. Roy Newell would be proud. And then, one evening, there is Roy Newell in our yard, giving Father a few more pointers.

"You'll need to aerate that lawn, Hal. Punch a bunch of holes in it. You can rent a machine that does the trick. Not too expensive, but it needs it. Lawns got to breathe, too. Maybe not now, but no longer than the spring next year."

"Next spring, then?"

"Yep. Next spring."

"What about the rose bush on the end of the house?"

"Aphids. Can see 'em from here."

"But I sprayed."

"They're pesky. Spray again. And I'd put in some fertilizer stakes next to your big fir tree out back. Won't make much difference this year, but it will next. Put 'em in at the drip line, that's where they go."

"Anything else I can do now? Anything that will spruce up the yard?"

Roy Newell smiles. "Expecting company, I'd say. Maggie and someone?"

A week passes, then it is almost the time for Maggie to arrive. Monday and Tuesday. Then Wednesday. It is a long drive from Utah to here, and we do not expect Maggie and Larry until . . . Maggie and Larry—the coupling seems odd; until now, its just been Maggie and Maggie only, my big sister . . . until close to dinner time.

Father comes home from work. He barely says hello to any of us. His mind is a trillion miles from here, but just where, I do not know. He paces. He walks into our yard, which has never looked better. Beautiful June day in Oregon, a yard that basks in full, golden sunlight. And Father kicks a few clods and sweeps away a little dirt and a few blades of shorn grass that have migrated onto the walkway to our front door.

He goes inside and when he comes out, he looks different than I have seen him before at this time of the day. Nice slacks, a pressed blue shirt, shined shoes.

To Claire, my senior sister by three years, I say, "What's Father so worried about? What's going on? I don't get it."

Claire says, "Don't you know anything? He's upset because Larry is coming to ask him if he can marry Maggie."

Maggie and Larry. Larry and Maggie. In times ahead, it will become Maggie-and-Larry and then MaggieandLarry, their names, their lives, their beings intertwined, a match, but more than a match. They become a pair. Later, they become one.

———

His car approaches, a brown 1964 Ford Falcon, and he pulls up to the curb with a flourish. Father, his arms folded, stares out through our living-room window. The young man Larry jumps from his car, rounds the rear of it, and holds open the door for Maggie. For the first time, Larry, the young man, the suitor, the one who has fallen in love with my sister and will care for her throughout his life and beyond, looks toward our house. Unseen by the would-be intruder, my father gazes at him, gazes down, steadiness in his eyes, unflinching. I am just to the side of Father, edging my way to the window so that I also can catch a glimpse of Larry, the young man, the young man who has captured my sister Maggie's heart. I also fold my arms and stare out through the front window. I look down, too. My father smells like strong aftershave, and his clothes give the air of crispness, like a fresh afternoon breeze.

Maggie-and-Larry walk toward the front door.

My father says, "He's a Ford man, I see."

Father preferred General Motors. Father never did like Fords. Chevys and Oldsmobiles, those were his cars.

———

We didn't know it then. We didn't know that the hinge of our world was swinging, and from that moment on, nothing in the Rogers family would ever be quite the same.

It is what happens when a family member separates, no matter the reason, no matter the noble intention responsible for the departure. Missions or marriage, military, or just to experience life on terms other than being in the shelter of home. When a family member leaves, nothing is the same. A certain, distinct sense of completeness flees as a brown dry leaf blown away by a strong west wind, and it can never be called back. Sons-in-law and daughters-in-law, and eventually, grandchildren may be added, but the sameness, the security, the satisfaction of knowing your children are under one roof—your roof—is gone. And so it was that the Rogers family was about to have an experience in seeing one of our own strike out on her own.

"It will not be the same here without her," Mother says one night, late, after Larry had arrived. She and Father are in their room, lights out, only quiet night noises about our house. Their eyes are open, I imagine, looking straight up at a dark ceiling. I hear them only because I cannot sleep and the room I share with my younger brother, Tom, is next to theirs.

"No, it won't. I knew it but I didn't know it. How are you supposed to know things like that?" my father says absently. "You don't, until it happens. You just don't."

Mother says, "I know, Hal. You don't know, do you? You don't."

He says, "You spend the first half of your adult life bringing them up and then you spend the second half watching them go away."

Mother says, "And the third half?" She giggles.

"Guess we'll see. But I like what the Church teaches about it."

"She's a good girl."

"Yes. She is. A good girl. They don't come better than our Maggie."

"He's fortunate."

"He is. He's lucky. Oh, how I will miss that girl of mine."

But we can't stand in the way of this migration of our own away from home. We can't. It would be wrong. We hold on to the plan, the thought, the belief, that we will all be united again, united in a way far beyond our earthly comprehension. More than just together, more than just close by. Different from any other relationship we have experienced on this earth. It is that thought that gets us by. It is the faith that allows us to take one tentative step after another until our footsteps become firm, until the next time the plan calls for us to go on an uncharted journey, when we leave with a trace more of confidence.

Just when "the talk" will take place is a mystery. Claire and I make a pact that we will keep our ears and eyes open and let each other know if anything out of the ordinary seems about to take place.

Larry has three days with us before he must leave for his own home. One day, two days. No talk yet. Maggie is still ours, not his, and he is still his own, not hers. Ours. Still ours.

Father is in the front yard. It is a beautiful day, soft and inviting, blue domed sky overhead, our verdant emerald lawn in front of us. The fragrance of fir and flower further dazzles our senses. Father looks east, toward Mt. Hood, its white snow cape and crooked south ridgeline serene in the morning sky.

Maggie and Larry. Maggie-and-Larry. MaggieandLarry.

I can hear my father's thoughts: *They are so young. What future do they have together?*

One more year of school. That would be nice. Maybe then. One more year, to have my own around me, that's all I ask. One more year. They don't have two nickels to rub together. They don't have a can of soup between them and no window to throw it out of. I can't help them in that way. I can't. I don't have much money myself. I don't. I can't help them. I will help them a little. I'll help all I can.

But they are crazy about each other. That counts, more than nickels, more than soup.

MaggieandLarry, MaggieandLarry.

———

This is not like making boxes at a factory, where you feed the fiber into the machine and the machine stamps out the box, perfect lines, perfect creases, right angles in a world that loves right angles. This is a part of life, a part of who you are and what you must experience, this is a part where you feel for the wind and set your sail and let the breeze take you wherever it may. And you can fight the breeze or you can let it blow you to the shore where you are supposed to land.

This is a part of the picture where God lets you put your experience and what you know and what you feel to work for you, and He steps back and thinks with lovingkindness, "All right. Show me. Prove to me. This is where I have given you the outline and now you fill it all in with the colors you select. It is your picture. It is your painting. You can choose the colors."

Larry walks by me.

"Morning, Neal."

"Hello, Larry."

That's all, he says no more, and he walks toward my father, hands plunged deep in pockets, his pace slow, deliberate, tense.

I think, *I need to go get Claire. I wonder where Tom is.*

"Morning, Brother Rogers."

"Morning, Larry."

"Nice day."

"Yes."

Words hang thick in the air. I can almost see them, falling forward from my father and from Larry, trying to gain flight like some ungainly bird, but falling, flapping to the ground, where they land, struggle, and die.

Larry says, "You sure have a nice yard. Really nice. You must work on it a lot."

For the first time, Father looks toward him.

"Why, thank you, Larry. It is a nice yard. My house isn't much, but we try to keep it clean and the yard looking nice. I have this friend, Roy, and . . . well, Roy. He knows yards."

"You'll have to tell me how you do it someday."

"I can. I can do that. I will. It's not hard, other than the first bit in the spring. A little fertilizer, a little trim work. There's some fertilizer made from fish, made in Alaska and it works real fine. Spray some now and again. Then it's just a matter of keeping it maintained. Helps to have a boy or two around for that. Maybe that's why I have sons."

These words do not fall on the ground. They stay airborne in the suddenly light, sweet early summer air.

Father is dressed as I have never seen him on a Saturday morning. He has on nice pants and a striped dress shirt and his Sunday shoes. I don't know why. Then I think I do.

It has something to do with a sense of history, family history, and years from now, when Larry recalls this moment, he will remember that my father looked nice for the occasion. And years from now, when Father recalls this moment, he will think, *I looked nice for the occasion.*

I think I need to go get Claire and tell her.

I run to the room she shares with my third sister, Rosie, and see that both of them are under their blankets, still asleep.

"Claire, I think they are going to have their talk. I think it's going to happen now. Father looks nice, and Larry is there, and this is the last day, and that's why I think they are going to talk."

From the next room over, I hear Mother and Maggie talking softly.

Claire sits up in bed and says, "Go spy on them. I'm not ready."

Father and his sense of history, his sense of presence, his sense of respectfulness and dignity. He wore nice clothes on the day that his future son-in-law asked him for his daughter.

So that when memory of days gone by and people gone by spark to life at some future time, there will be a sense of rightness and purposefulness and honor to it all.

I quickly walk back to the front porch. The conversation between my father and Larry seems earnest. Unobtrusively, I sit on the front porch, their backs to me, their voices steady. I am a good spy. They do not even know I am there.

"We have plans, Brother Rogers."

"So I gather."

"We have talked a lot. We think it can work."

"Yes, it is one of the blessings of being young. Thinking it all can work."

Father looks up in the sky. Far overhead, a jet plane leaves a contrail, thin at first, then widening to fill a portion of the vast blue. Then he suddenly wheels around and sees me quietly listening on the stairway.

I am a spy who is caught in the act.

"Let's go some place where we can talk," Father says, and Larry nods nervously. The big moment is at hand for him. His future, short-term and far into incalculable infinities, is about to take a turn. He has never faced such a moment.

They walk to the driveway and climb into the Oldsmobile.

So this sense of honor. I look back now, and this box-maker—a man who worked with his hands, who never attended a day of college, who lived a simple, productive, and good life, who simply went about doing good—he climbed into a car, out of earshot.

Ten years after he passed on, a woman came up to me at the end of a session of stake conference.

"You are the son of Hal Rogers?"

"Yes, I am."

"I want to tell you something. You do not know my name."

She is, I would guess, in her middle forties, plainly dressed, green-eyed, a slight blush, determined in manner and voice.

"I was in your ward when your father was bishop, after your mission. I had some problems. They were . . ." and her eyes wander, as though looking at someone behind me, "substantial problems. I had to repent. You know where it all led and what I needed to do. You know that. Your father was so kind that night, his counselors, too. At that point in my life, I didn't much care for men, especially men with authority. I didn't know what to expect. They listened. But it was so very difficult. The hardest thing I've had to do, ever."

"You don't need to say anything more. Please."

"But I will. I need to say this. There is something important I need to say. I want you to know something. At the end, when it was all over and the prayer was finished, your father said, 'May I escort you to your car?'

"No single gesture has meant so much to me in my entire life. We walked to my car, down a dark corridor, to the parking lot, and he was saying little things to encourage me the whole way, to give me hope for my future. He even got me to smile. It was my personal turning point. He would not allow me to walk alone at that time. Do you understand? Do you see? *He would not let me walk alone.* Had I walked away alone that night, I probably wouldn't be here today."

Then she turned abruptly and strode away, and I have

never seen her again, but I have thought often of what she said and how she felt and how she looked, and what it is to be an honorable man, what it is to make boxes.

―――――

Mother comes to the porch where I am sitting and joins me on the steps, my mission doomed. She says, "Where are they? Where are your father and Larry?"

I point to the car and she looks startled. Then Father motions for her to come to the car. She rises from the steps and walks to the car and Larry hops into the backseat and Mother gets in the front seat, and I doubt a stranger setting for a talk of this nature has ever occurred.

Claire comes to the front door and peers through the screen.

"Well?"

"They're in the car."

"The car?"

"Look for yourself. They're in the car."

"Oh, poor Maggie!"

They were in the car for another half hour. When they emerged, there was an air of lightness. Things had gone well. Larry looked happy. Father and Larry shook hands and then gave each other an awkward, male-typical embrace, and then Larry went into the house and Mother and Father just stood on the lawn and talked quietly, though excitedly, for a few minutes.

Plans were being hatched. Plans were in the air. Another year would have been nice, but when you know, you know, and when it is right, it is right, and there isn't any good reason, especially not reasons of dollars and cents, to put off what this life and the first of the next of many eternities hold for you. Our steps to the eternities are generally small and measured, but, occasionally, there comes a great leap, and for MaggieandLarry, this was such a jump.

MaggieandLarry soon came to the front door and quickly got into the old Falcon and drove away. We didn't see them again until afternoon.

In the air, the jet was long gone, but the wide, fluffy wake of the contrail could be seen to the horizon.

The wedding and sealing was in Oakland, the nearest temple to us in those days. I don't remember much. A long drive. The wait in the room inside the temple. The people were nice. We ate at the Wharf when the ceremony was over, and the waiter undercharged us on purpose. The clear skies, cool breeze, coming in off the Bay. The air smelled of salt. I watched big ships move slowly under the Bay bridge and foamy whitecaps thrash the pilings under the pier.

See him? Center field. It's Willie Mays. Finest ballplayer alive today. One of the best ever.

We are at Candlestick Park, seated behind third base, maybe twenty rows up, the day before the sealing. Father, Larry, Tom, and me.

"We've come all this way. Might as well see Willie Mays," Father says. "Kind of a bonus to it all. Maggie gets married and we see Willie Mays play center field. Two good things."

And soon after that, we are standing in a line in the small, pretty room, off the chapel of the Harrison Street building. It is where MaggieandLarry had their reception, where people came to honor them. We stood in front of the marble fireplace—my father, brother, and I in our white dinner jackets, Mother in a gold dress, my two sisters as bridesmaids, dressed in pink.

And MaggieandLarry in the center, young, fresh, a pretty life just ahead of them, waiting to be lived, to be experienced.

We are practical people in my family. When the last of the guests left the church, we all went out to the car and got our work clothes. We came back into the church and went to the restrooms to change our clothes and begin the chore of taking down the decorations, folding the chairs, and putting away the tables, cleaning the kitchen, and sweeping the floor. Roy Newell came by a little after eleven, unasked, after having come through the line three hours earlier. With no more than a quick greeting, he pulled a long table onto its side, slid the bracket down the channel, kicked in the legs, and hefted the table onto a cart, a routine known well by many generations of priesthood holders.

Roy stayed until the end, close to two in the morning, then locked up the building.

Father tried to hand him twenty dollars, but the look on Roy Newell's face was blunt and sure, and Father folded the bill back into his wallet. Father didn't often retreat.

"Well. What a day. What a long day. It was so much work, but I think Maggie appreciated it." We are driving home in our Oldsmobile. My mother leans her head against Father's right shoulder and yawns. Claire and Tom are in the backseat with me. My youngest sister, Rosie, curls in Mother's lap. Father shakes his head. "She wanted to stay behind and help clean up. On her night. Imagine that. She's a good one, our Maggie."

And then he stops and thinks, and I am sure he is realizing that the pronoun he just used—*our*—has taken on a new meaning.

Maggie and Larry. Maggie-and-Larry. MaggieandLarry and-the-rest-of-us-too. They have become "ours" not "mine." We are ours.

"Understand, Claire. Nothing from you like this for at least three years. It will take us that long to recover," Father says dreamily. "Three years, minimum. Five or six would be better."

"Listen to your father," my mother says, barely above a whisper, her thoughts drowsy, fuzzy, fluttering far above the earth somewhere.

"You don't need to worry about me," Claire says. "I don't like boys. Not at all. Except for you, Daddy."

Claire, that night barely eighteen, would herself be engaged within a year, married the next.

Father sighs. "And I got to see Willie Mays. Not a bad few days."

CHAPTER 12

June 1971

Things are changing in our neighborhood. Maggie is married. Robin Mitchell Hutchins is a mother. Billy Crosby, a boy a few years older than I who lived three doors down, goes away on a baseball scholarship to a school in California and comes home one weekend married to a pretty girl named Gayle. My father's hair begins to gray. Mother's normal frenetic pace begins to slow. Tom gets one of the lead roles in his school production of *Our Town*. Rosie enters middle school. And the tide of change would soon draw me into its current and pull me away, too.

The box factory is no more, my sister Claire tells me. She says, "We were passing through, heading to Vancouver, and we drove right by where it was. I looked off the Interstate and it was gone. So much of our history, so many hours of our father's life, and it is all gone. I thought about getting off and finding our old house, but we didn't. We didn't want to get caught in the traffic. We had reservations in Bellingham. They're turning it into some kind of condo-and-shopping complex—the box factory and the buildings near it. Most of the old buildings are gone, or remodeled so that they don't look the same. I heard they're asking $500,000 for those condos, and they're the cheap ones. What would our father say!

"And they called it a container plant the last few years. Containers. Not boxes, not what they were. Containers. What a funny name. Imagine Father and what he would say. 'I am a container-maker.' No, not our father. Not Dad."

I continued playing baseball—through Little League, then Babe Ruth, then high school and American Legion ball. I grew a couple of more inches, a shade under six feet by then, and my arms were long and sinewy. I played center field, like Mays and Mantle. And like my father

The first letter from a college baseball team arrived in the mail just before my junior year in high school.

Claire, again. "Do you know only one ward meets in that building now? The old building on Harrison? I was in town a couple of months ago and I stopped by. They consolidated the wards. No more First Ward, no more Twelfth Ward. They call it the Colonial Heights Ward. That's what it was back before, back before all the wards were just numerals. The membership numbers weren't there any more. Everyone lives in the suburbs. I hope they never sell that church. It still looks good. The lawn is so green, just like when Brother Newell was there. So pretty. Just sitting there, on that little rise, just like when we were kids."

In the neighborhood once, many years ago, when we were finishing a baseball game on a lazy summer night, a group of fathers gathered to watch the end of our contest. One of the fathers—I can't remember who—said something about boxes and how it must be easy to make boxes. "You adjust the machine, feed in the cardboard, and the rest is all pretty automatic, right, Hal? Don't you ever get bored making boxes?"

Father smiled dreamily and said, "Oh, it's a little more complicated than that. Never been bored yet. Don't expect to be, either."

At dinner the next night, my father says, out of the blue, "Lets talk about boxes. I've been thinking a lot about boxes. Did you know boxes aren't actually made of cardboard?"

Time accelerates. My senior year in high school flutters by. I sign a letter of intent to play center field at a university. I read about myself in a scouting report: "Fine arm, good instincts, great on the base paths, smart player. Runs well. Not much of a power hitter. Good on a two-strike count, chokes up and always makes contact. If he adds twenty pounds, he'll be a complete player."

I also accept a job working on a Forest Service wildfire crew in eastern Oregon, starting the week after my high school graduation. My new baseball coach isn't pleased with that decision, he'd rather I hooked up with a local team and played ball all summer, but the money from firefighting will be useful. "Come back in the fall in good shape," the coach says. "Work out on your own, keep in shape. Run up those mountains and put on a few extra pounds of muscle."

"I will," I tell him. And I do.

"Boxes are not shipped in boxes, did you know that, Neal? Kind of odd, when you think about it."

Father walks through the box plant. My high school graduation is over, and I have a few days before I report to the fire crew. He wanted me to come to his workplace. I wanted to be here. He walks briskly. The workers in the box plant call to him. He smiles and greets them and waves his hand.

"It's different now than when I started. Someday, they'll use computers to design the boxes. Big computers that take up a room the size of a closet. It'll be more complex, but it's more efficient. You can make boxes different ways but they always come out about the same, if you do it right. And we recycle so much, which we didn't do when I started in this business. Use it once, use it again. Makes good sense to me. I started out feeding the web onto the corrugating rolls. It's about the most basic job there is here. But what comes out of it is worth it."

He loves this place. He loves the pungent smell of pulp and paper and glue. He loves the machinery, the glue machines, the die-cut machines, the rotary die cutter. He loves what is produced: boxes made to order, constructed at precise right angles, stronger than you would think. He loves the grit of this dusty old plant. He loves to run his fingers across the paper ridges of the fluted boxes. He loves the noise of the forklifts, their grinding little engines, the toot of their horns. He loves to see the boxes on the floor, stacked on pallets, ready for shipping. He loves the language of boxmakers: *singleface, single wall, triple wall, flutes.*

He loves to hear people call his name as he strolls through with his eldest son: "Hello, Hal. Got the boy with you today, I see. Think he'll go to work here someday?"

And my father always replying jovially, "Nope. Neal here has too many brains. He's a college man. He'll go a lot further than his dad. Gonna play baseball in college, how about that?"

And their mocking, good-natured replies: "Well, it won't take much to outdo his old man."

We walk through the door into his small office. He closes the door behind him, and the happy din from the plant floor turns to a soft hum.

"You know, it's funny. Most people think that boxes are made of cardboard, but they're not. You think you know something as basic as that, that a box is made from cardboard, and it's not. You can get fooled by a lot of simple things, can't you?"

He pulls his chair from behind his desk and motions for me to take my place on a nearby folding chair. He reaches for his brown bag and pulls out two sandwiches. "Mom packed a second sandwich. She figured you might be here about noon. Lunch for two." He hands me one of the sandwiches. "Let me run down to the vending machine and get us some cartons of milk to wash this all down with," and before I can agree or not, he's up and moving through the door.

The roar of the machinery briefly rolls into the office before the door closes behind him. As he disappears around the corner, his hand shoots up in the air, acknowledging the call of a fellow worker.

My father makes boxes for a living. He will put all five children through college on a boxmaker's wages.

While waiting for him to return, I stand up, my sandwich in hand, and stare through the window of his door to the production floor below. Machines clanking, big rolls of paperboard being swallowed up on the corrugating line, stacks of flattened boxes rolling down a conveyor.

The evening before I leave for my job in eastern Oregon. I spend it packing and thinking about what it means to leave my home and my family. This is, I understand, the end of one era, the beginning of another. I saw it with Maggie-and-Larry. From the moment I kiss my mother good-bye and get into the Oldsmobile and begin the long drive to a tiny town in the Blue Mountains, something will change, and the change will be irrevocable. Whenever I come home from this point on, it will be as a visitor.

My father looks at me wistfully as I lug the old duffel bag out of my room, filled with what I think I'll need to be a firefighter.

"Got everything, Neal?"

"I think so."

"Your boots. They'll be important to you. Take good care

of them. Good thing you've had a couple of weeks to break them in."

"I think they'll be fine. I'll get a lot of use out of them."

He looks out the front window. The sun is about an hour from setting.

"One more time. Neal, can we go into the yard and play catch one more time? I'd like to do that."

"Sure, Dad. Once more. It will be fun. I'd like to do that, too. Like old times."

All those hours playing baseball on our street, all the Little League and Legion and high school games, but it all really started with me and my father lobbing the ball back and forth to each other. I never gave him credit. There were times, many times, when he must have been tired and not felt like playing catch, times when his muscles ached from a hard day at work, times when he had other things he wanted to do. But from the time I was little, I can hardly ever remember him turning down a game of catch. He's the one who taught me how to push off my right foot when making a long throw toward home. He's the one who taught me to choke up on the bat when the count was two strikes against me. He's the one who taught me how to read a batter's swing and shade one way or another when I played center field.

The lawn is lush, green and deep.

In the twilight, we toss the ball to each other, back and forth, back and forth, and I try to avoid this thought: *Tomorrow, I leave home.*

We ate the sandwiches that Mom prepared. I shook my father's hand. I looked him square into his eyes. I noticed how much more gray there was in his hair, how his shoulders were slightly hunched. His grip was still strong, but not as strong as it once had been, and I thought, *Time is a bandit.* I thanked him for seeing me, for taking the time to show me around once more. On my way out, I nodded and smiled and waved to a couple of the workmen. I wanted them to think that Hal Rogers's son was a lot like Hal Rogers. Then I left. That June day was the last time I was ever in the box plant.

He was right. There is more than you'd think to making boxes.

My father and his boxes—his family, his honor, his integrity, his good name, his wisdom.

Does my life pass in faintness or strength? And I still ask the question that every son of every good man must ask: How do I compare with my father? Have I made good boxes, too?

Dad and Tom drove me to the little town where I would spend my summer. I don't remember much about the trip, other than thinking that maybe I could come home over the Fourth of July weekend. We stopped in Pendleton to get a bite to eat. Once we arrived at the ranger district, my father stayed only long enough to make sure I had a bunk in the crew quarters and all my gear was stowed. He pushed a ten-dollar bill into my hand, gave me a hug, wished me luck.

He told Tom it was time, time to get into the car and make the long trip back to Portland. It was four o'clock in the afternoon, and he wanted to be on the road. He was going to work the next day.

Tommy got into the car next to him. Father rolled down his window and looked at me.

"When you get two strikes on you, Neal, you know what to do."

"Yes, I know what to do. Choke up on the bat and make contact."

"That's right. Good-bye, son."

I remember what he said about making boxes.

"You know, it's funny. Most people think that boxes are made of cardboard, but they're not. You think you know something as basic as that, that a box is made from cardboard but that's not the case. It's a surprise to most people, a real surprise, and they kind of feel disappointed, I think. Disappointed about it all. They think they know all there is to know about boxes and then they find out they don't."

You start off with so many dreams and you know where you want to go, and then you wake up one day and find out that where you're going to end up is not where you thought you might be. You thought you would make boxes, but the boxes never got made, or the boxes were weak or didn't fold properly or didn't hold when the load they were asked to bear collapsed them. I can't make boxes the way my father did.

"Neal's a college man. He'll go a lot further than his dad. I'm glad that he got the chance to do some of the things I never did. Darn proud of him, yes I am."

He was wrong about that. *It's the one thing he was wrong about.* Honor in life comes from more than what you do to earn a living, more than what you desire to be. Too many men and women aspire to be great but can't or won't do great things. They look above when greatness is just below them. They measure greatness in things and not in quiet deeds. My father may have been trying to teach his eldest son that he would find greatness at his feet and greatness at his door, not in the moon, the stars, the sky overhead, in title or position, the black bottom line, or beckoning bright lights. Greatness is found in small, simple, sturdy good deeds, repeated over and over.

His greatness was found in each box he made.

"You can do better, Neal. Better than ending up in a dusty old plant like I did, just scraping along. Oh, we never lacked for anything, but we had some lean times, although I hope you kids didn't notice and I don't think you did. More hamburger than steak, that's for sure. But you'll do better, Neal. You've got the talent, you've got the drive."

But I haven't gone further than my father. With all he taught me, with all the advantages I had, I cannot. The universal question that every son has about his father: *Will I be as good a man as he was?* In my case, I understand the answer is no. No, at least for now. But I have a star overhead to guide me.

So I sit, not at a computer, but at an old Underwood typewriter and peck out this story about my father, the boxmaker. Maybe, in my life, I feel as though I've taken two strikes and it's now time to choke up on the bat and just make contact. Maybe my desire to write a book about fathers and sons is the best I can do to pass on what I have seen, what I have experienced, what I have learned.

The Underwood belonged to my father. My mother once told me that when he was young, my dad would come down to the basement and sit at the typewriter and type things—stories, poems, letters, thoughts. I was surprised. I never knew. I sit at a computer all day at work and spend most of my time writing, but at night, at home, I peck out my words on my father's old Underwood. It is a small way to show him honor. It helps me to feel closer to him.

We never found anything that he wrote, although my mother and I spent hours in the basement looking for any of his papers. I would give almost anything to read a story or a poem written by my dad, even a letter. I worry that his story will melt away with the passing of a single generation.

I will not allow my father nor the boxes he made to be forgotten.

CHAPTER 13

A work conference ended on a Saturday afternoon in Newport, a town on the Oregon coast. As soon as I read the e-mail telling me about it, I began to do the calculations. It would be so easy to drive from there to Portland, spend the night, and walk up the stairs to the beautiful old chapel on Sunday morning. I had not attended a sacrament meeting there for almost twenty years.

"I could fly back the following day, after going to church. It would be so easy," I tell Amanda. "I doubt anyone would remember me or recognize me. Most of the people who knew me growing up have probably moved long ago or passed on. They'd be in their seventies or eighties. But the memories of that building, and the chance to walk up and down my old street. I would like that. I would like that very much."

"Go ahead. We'll be fine here an extra day."

"I think I will. It won't be too expensive. I'll find a place to stay and book my return trip for Monday morning."

"You should do it, Neal. What a chance for you. I know you've been thinking a lot about your father and mother, the neighborhood, the old church. They all hold so much meaning for you. We'll be fine here."

"I'll go then. You're right. It's too good a chance to pass up."

The messages were vague at first. Mother would say, "Oh, he's tired. That's all. That's all I think it is. I hope that's all it is."

"You're sure?"

"Yes, I'm sure. Pretty sure, anyway. He sees the doctor in a few weeks for a physical, but I may push him in sooner than that. But you know your dad. He'd rather do almost anything than go see a doctor. He's stubborn."

"When he feels better, come to Salt Lake City and spend some time with us. The kids would love to see their grandparents. You haven't seen our new house yet."

"Sure, yes. Sure. When he's better. When he's got some pep back. Yes, we'll come."

"We'd like that."

I wonder about him. He finally left the box plant, and when he did, there was little for him at home. All five us were gone. On the few occasions when I visited, he seemed almost ill at ease in his own home, in his own company.

"Nothing, nothing at all. I'm fine. Just restless, I reckon. You live your life like chapters in a book, and I've closed one chapter and don't know where to begin the next," he says. "Funny thing is, I don't know whether I'm a writer or just a reader in this book." He pauses, then starts again. "I know I get on your mother's nerves sometimes," he says with a sly grin.

From the next room, my mother calls, "On my nerves *sometimes?* Try all the time, Hal."

"Joy, I beg your indulgence and forgiveness. But we've been together this long, and I am too old to change. You're stuck with me, dear."

His hair, always full, is now almost all silver. His eyelids seem to droop a little. He is quieter than before. He goes to the temple twice a week, works in his yard. His twenty-year-old car is spotless, waxed, runs as though it were new off the showroom floor. He talks, elbows on the top of the fence, about the weather with his neighbor, Mr. Teuscher. One day, he gathers up Mother and they drive to the coast, eat good clam chowder and fresh salmon. They feel the ocean breeze on their faces and hold hands on a long walk down the stony beach. But he is so exhausted that Mother drives them home. It is a first. I cannot remember a time when Father let Mother drive on a trip home.

The early afternoon sunshine flows through the window of the living room in our modest home. His head nods, he dozes. He wakes up for a few seconds and apologizes: "Sorry, Neal. You've come all this way and I can't keep my eyes open. Getting old, I guess. Sorry. Let me close my eyes and sleep just for a few minutes, then we'll go do something. When you were little, we'd always find a good place to play. Let me rest, then we'll find someplace new to play."

Mother looks toward me, lines sunk around her eyes and creasing her forehead, worry etched on her face.

This is a book, he said, a book with chapters. Finish one, start another, until all the chapters have been read.

With a chill and a shudder, with a knot in my stomach and with a sense of things done too soon, I understand why my dad cannot find the next chapter to read.

My conference ends, and I begin the drive to Portland, the drive home, along crooked Highway 101, spectacular vistas of the ocean connecting the small towns, with the souvenir shops, restaurants, salt-water taffy stores lining the main road. The drive takes me almost four hours before I pull up in front of the hotel where I will spend Saturday evening, in preparation for a visit Sunday morning to my original home ward.

She phones. "Your father. I think you should come home now, Neal."

Words I have dreaded for a year.

"How bad is he?"

"You should come home now because he can still talk and he will recognize you. This is the time you should come home."

Her voice is tired, her voice is flat, her voice is beautiful in its calmness and fortitude. I think, *We are a strong people, we are a strong family. We are the boxes he made. We will get through this because he made us strong, and we can bear whatever weight is placed upon us.*

"Claire is coming tonight. MaggieandLarry are already

here. Tom should be here tomorrow afternoon. Rosie already is."

"Are you okay, Mom?"

Her calm voice is clear, stronger than just an instant before.

"Yes. I am. Come home, Neal. It's time. You need to come home."

I look out through my hotel window and see the creamy outline of Mt. Hood, sixty miles to the east. There is a park across the street, and I stroll toward it as the sun settles beyond the west hills. It is a beautiful late spring evening. Children run and romp on the grassy green slopes, while adults wander among the park's rosebushes. There is a friendly, warm chatter in the air. Farther away, down the grassy slope, I see children on the swing sets, their parents gently nudging them forward. A raven caws, hushing for a moment the songs of robins and the one quick call of a western meadowlark.

In the far corner of the park, I see young boys with bats, balls, and gloves. In the diminishing light, I hear one of them call out, "Game. Too dark to see now. I gotta go home anyway."

It gladdens me, makes this trip feel more right, that boys still play baseball in my hometown.

"Hello, Neal. Glad you could come."

Father greets me as though he were welcoming a long overdue soul to sacrament meeting. Gracious to the end.

With bravado and a false face, I smile and say, "Hey, Pops. Of course I would come. Mom said we were having a little family party. I couldn't miss out on that."

He is at home, in his bed. It has been six months since I have last seen him. His condition has deteriorated, his features yellowish, large dark spots on his hands and arms, his face sunken, his breath coming in long, slow whooshes, labored.

"Some party."

"Better than no party at all."

"I suppose you are right about that, son. I hope I can stay awake for it. Sure do sleep a lot these days. Don't like it much."

"You will. You're too tough and too stubborn to miss out on a party being thrown in your honor."

He smiles and closes his eyes. I reach for his hand and hold it. He falls asleep, and I sit there with him for two hours, holding his hand, listening to him breathe, and running my other hand lightly over his forehead, his shoulder, his arm.

I can do no more.

I return to my hotel and spend a fitful night, hardly sleeping. I'm too excited. In the morning, I rise, get cleaned up, put on my best blue suit and begin the drive across town to the chapel. My car almost seems to know the way. It winds down through the southwest part of the city, finds its way through the loops and tunnels, the one-way streets and approaches the lap of the Ross Island Bridge. Across the river, down a side street. Up to Harrison Boulevard, a right turn, and in twenty more minutes I'll be at the old chapel of stone.

He awakes. "You're still here? How long have I been asleep?"

"Not long, Dad. Not long at all. I might have dozed a little myself."

"How nice of you to come. Did I say that to you before?"

"Nope. Wouldn't miss it, Dad. When you get better, we can toss the ball around. If you take it easy on me. Did I tell you that Jeremy is the starting shortstop on his freshman team?"

"No, I don't think you did. Doesn't surprise me, though. I'd like to watch him play sometime. He takes after you. Shortstop, you say. It's a good position."

I continue to rub his arm, his forehead, his shoulders, his chest. I want to touch him. I want to squeeze his hand and say things to him that he will remember, that he will cherish, that will cause him to, in some way, feel better, be lightened.

Many of the houses look the same as they did a generation ago. I can almost see the people who inhabited them—people working in their yards, tilling their gardens, touching up the paint, grabbing the newspaper from their front porch, gathered around admiring a new car. I can almost see young fathers and mothers with the old-fashioned baby buggies pushing along the sidewalk on a Sunday morning stroll. I can see the families filing toward their cars, the girls in pink or yellow dresses, the boys in their white shirts and little bow ties, solemnly getting in and heading to church. The trees we climbed, the bushes where we hid for games of kick-the-can. The old neighborhood still looks pretty good. There's the telephone pole. We used to lay one of our gloves parallel to it and that would be home base. The other telephone pole, maybe forty yards away, was the imaginary homerun wall. Telephone pole to telephone pole. Hit it past the pole, and it's a home run. Double or nothing, you had to get to second base or you were out. My house looks about the same. Still painted white, the lawn verdant. I wonder who lives there. They've kept it up.

It's all so familiar, so good. I'll come back to this neighborhood after church and take that long slow walk up the street. I'll softly call out the names of the people who lived in each home and wish the voices of ghosts would call back to me. But for now, I need to get to church. Sacrament meeting starts in fifteen minutes.

I watch my father as he falls into a light sleep, and I think about boxes. At this bedside, caressing the old man's hand, I have a vision: A large bright warehouse, miles long and miles wide and it is filled with boxes—big boxes, little boxes, all kinds of boxes. Not flattened boxes, but formed boxes, standing straight, stiff, erect and strong, one on top of another, layer after layer, no two boxes exactly alike, but all fitting together perfectly. I understand this vision. It represents what my father did with his life. He made boxes. My father, the boxmaker.

He closes his eyes. Then he opens them, and the faintest of smiles appears on his face and, for a moment, his eyes dazzle.

"Dad, the look on your face. What are you thinking about, Dad?"

"I am thinking about you and what I've done in this life."

Does he understand? Does he understand why I have come to love the boxes he made?

"I wish I could make boxes, Dad. I'd like to make boxes, like you. The boxes you made are wonderful. The boxes you made are beautiful. They are pretty boxes, Dad."

His eyes are wide open, the corners of his mouth curl upward, sweetly, peacefully. Then he says, one word uttered at a time, each followed by a pause, each carrying the gravity of the world as a wise man has seen it.

"Oh, Neal, but you can make boxes. Someday you'll understand. That's what you've never known about yourself. You can make boxes, too."

The streets between my old house and the church are familiar, almost as though I'd never left. Then I see it, on the grassy knoll.

The old stone chapel looks beautiful on this bright spring day. I notice how the stones are cut into squares, how the mortar between them holds them in place, gathered together, laid a stone at a time, with a larger plan guiding every step of the way, all joining to form a perfect symmetry to this fine old building. The square stones, lovingly laid in place, look to me like boxes.

My father is sitting up in bed now. He seems more alert, lighter. The nap has done him some good. He even tries to gag down one of those milkshakes in a can, something the doctor said would be good for him. I do not want to lose this man. I cannot lose this man. I am not ready to try to make boxes the way he did.

I hear a doorbell, the voices, the clatter, the footsteps coming down the hallway. Rose, MaggieandLarry, coming back from a quick errand, buying groceries for Mother, returning with something for lunch.

He nods at me. "Every father wants his son to be better than him. In my mind, there's no doubt you're a few steps ahead of me, Neal."

Before I can tell him no, that's not the way it is, Rosie comes in and throws her arms around me. MaggieandLarry follow close behind. I glance and I catch his eye. I want to believe what he said about my ability to create boxes, about my ability to equal him. It was spoken as a promise to me and a son always remembers his father's promises. They never go away. He knows my concern and he looks at me firmly as Rosie makes a fuss over him, and he nods almost imperceptibly.

And in that nod and the look in his eye, I understand that he is fine, just fine, with what is taking place. He is tired now. His head droops a little as Rosie and MaggieandLarry gather around him, but he remains cheerful and gladly endures our chatter. But he knows. Yes, he knows.

He has crafted his last box.

I drive by the building once, then turn around and drive by it again. I drive behind it, through the parking lot. It looks good. Age has only increased its beauty. The lawn is green, and I hope boys still play steal-the-flag on it. Roy Newell would be pleased.

This building of stone and rose, it was where the services took place. It was on a spring day, much like this, when the flowers were just beginning to bud.

Bishop Ranstrom spoke, and so did Roy Newell. Sister Palmer came back to Portland and sang "O My Father," Dad's favorite hymn. Sister Austin, brushing close to eighty years, was there, a determined glint in her eye, a mission at hand. Later, she would orchestrate the family supper. The neighbors, so many of the neighbors, their faces older, somber. Tullers. Hendersons. Baileys. Martinos. Rowans. Barneys. Nelsons. Rosas. Seiji Inahara flew all the way from Sapporo. Robert Blue was there. Jim and Sandy Smart, both now graying and plump, sat solemnly in almost the same place they had on that eventful Sunday so many years before. Their children, I heard said, are brilliant.

And people from the plant, where the boxes were made, they showed up, too. One of them later told me that the place was shut down for two hours by the new general manager, an old friend of Dad's, so that everyone could come to the services. They came in their work clothes, some with a few ties awkwardly hitched to the collars of their plain work shirts. They came in sturdy work boots. They came in jeans and they came in tennis shoes. They came in tee-shirts, a few of the women came in skirts. They were dusty, they had nicks and scars on their hands. They came to honor my father, the man who taught them how to make boxes. They showed up, all of them. The whole plant. A new generation of boxmakers.

At the end, when I stood up to leave and follow the casket out to the parking lot, I took Mother by her arm and then looked back and saw that the chapel was full and more, and that the old wood partition had had to be lifted, to allow people to spill over into the cultural hall to accommodate all who attended.

For some reason, the image I'd had a week before of the long, wide warehouse came to mind, the image filled with innumerable boxes, beautiful in their simplicity and elegant in their design. I'd like to build boxes. I have wanted to ever since I was a little boy.

———

I drove back to the front of the church and found a place to park on the street. I had a few minutes left before I needed to go in. I watched people, young, old, and in between, walk up the stone stairs to the wide wood doors and walk in. Outside, only a few clouds drifted by, high overhead. The fragrance in the air was of fir trees and flowers budding, freshly mowed lawn, and the fecundity of newly turned soil. The cupped petals of roses, red, pink, and yellow, reached toward heaven.

———

In the garage of the house where I grew up. Outside, a cool, rainy October day in Oregon. She sits on a metal folding chair in the doorway from the house to the garage, dressed in a green sweatshirt with a hood, pulled up around her, to keep her from the cold. She wears thick, black pants, wool socks, and walking shoes. An old radio plays classical music. She shivers. I pick up a box and peer inside, old magazines.

"These need to go, Mom. You can't keep these old magazines. You don't look at them any more, do you? They should go. They're very old, frayed, you'll never read them."

"No, no I don't read them. You're right, Neal. I guess they could go. They are such nice magazines. I kept them for so many years. You kids used to cut them up and use them in your school reports."

Her garage has filled up with things, especially since Father's passing. She can't seem to part with anything. I have come back to her house for a weekend to help her clear space, so that she can again fit her car in. A cold, wet Oregon winter is coming; she will need to put her car in the garage.

The radio music, Vivaldi, I think, bounces along, thin and spry.

I take the magazines and place them in a box that will end up on the curb and be taken away in another day.

From nowhere, Mother says, "He worried the most about you, Neal, but he also said you were the most like him. He was proud to have you as his son."

I pretend not to hear her. I take another load of old magazines and place them in another box. I look around and see big plastic jars filled with small things—rusty nails, old broken tools, yellowed newspaper clippings, bolts, nuts and screws, parts, parts of things that don't add up to anything at all.

"I think these can go."

"All right. They can go."

I grab the plastic jars and place them in yet another box.

She says, "It wasn't Tom, it wasn't the girls. It was you that he saw himself in the most. I don't think you knew how much he loved you, your brother, and the girls."

I brush the grime off my hands. I find an old towel and wipe my hands clean.

"I never had far to look for a hero."

Had I ever called Father my hero? I turn my attention to the things in front of me.

"Another half hour and we'll be able to get your car in, Mom. We're a good team. Rosie said we'd never get it done."

"Rosie was wrong. We'll make sure to tell her."

She shudders again. The damp cold. I'd forgotten how cold it gets in Oregon, when the rain falls and the wind blows, and the clouds seem to smother the earth. It could be half the temperature in Utah and still not as cold as it is in Oregon when it rains.

"You'd better go in, Mom. It's too cold out. I'll take care of it from here."

She rises from the folding chair. "Maybe I will go in. You're almost done."

She turns and takes a step toward her house.

"You, Neal. It was you, the most like him. We used to talk about it often, when we couldn't sleep at night. You two. I look at you now and see your father as he was thirty years ago. But you are also the most like him in personality and outlook on life."

I tell her, "I guess so. Maybe. I know it, Mom."

He was my hero. I never told him. I hope he just knew it. People use the word *hero* too much. In my case, I didn't use it enough. All I needed was to say it once—to the person for whom it would matter the most.

Then I softly slide a pair of boxes aside, filled with parts of things, where they won't be in her way.

I have envisioned this moment: I will stroll up the stone walk, climb the stairs, and swing wide-open the wood doors. I will close my eyes for a second or two and breathe deeply and walk in, back through time, back through the years. I will look for the painting of the Good Shepherd, leading His sheep and holding a lamb in the back of the chapel.

I climb out of my car and take measured, steady steps up the walkway. I look up at the entrance to the building, my eyes trying to drink in each second of this experience. Slowly, each step measured, I walk up the stone stairway. Halfway up, I become aware of two people ascending slowly toward the door, speaking in calm, low voices, just ahead of me.

He is an older gentleman. As I catch up to them, he holds the door open for, first, his wife, and second for me.

My eyes and his eyes lock in gaze, and a slow, crinkly smile spreads across his face.

In a voice as gentle as a mother to her newborn, he says:

"Welcome, Neal. I've wondered about you these many years. I remember you and remember your father well. He made boxes for a living, didn't he? He was a good man.

I hoped you would come back some day. I imagine you are a lot like your father. You favor him. Welcome, son, welcome."

It is Bishop Ranstrom at the door, holding it open, inviting me home.

Then I begin to understand. I have tried to do what I saw my father do. And for me, that is enough. I may never match up to him, his deeds, the people he helped, his wisdom and his kindness, his depth of love for people, but what I have done is good, it is acceptable. I tried.

Standing there on the steps of the old church building, close to the place I grew up in, I can almost see the faces of a thousand people I have known, I have helped, I have loved. I have a legacy. This is what it will be. This is what it is like. The triumph over ourselves, through Him, the return to our long-sought home in peace, saying, *This is what I have done, may I enter?*

Bishop Ranstrom raises his eyes toward me, expecting me to say something.

How can I explain to him all that I feel, all that seems to have come together and converged at this tender moment, at this place? I can only tell him this one thing, curious as it sounds.

"I can make boxes."

He nods. He knows. He also has made boxes. We share something in common, as do all who humbly follow. Our sturdy lives, square corners. The greatness we see when we bow our heads. The Savior was a carpenter. I think He made boxes. I can also build beautiful things.

My father once told me, I like people who try.

I am a boxmaker, too.